"Mutt heard the girl screaming from next door."

It wasn't quite an accusation, but it came pretty close. Jody couldn't afford for this cop to report back to CPS that she wasn't providing adequate care for Mia.

"She does that at night, but we're trying to work through it."

When Mia smiled at the shepherd, Jody's heart did a stutter step. "Don't take this the wrong way, but is he friendly? Your dog, I mean."

The deputy glanced down at his companion. "Mutt recently retired from the K-9 patrol. The only time he's spent around kids was when he used to do community events. He was always patient with them."

Mutt left his owner to join Mia, laying his huge head in her lap. That brought another smile to the little girl's face.

The deputy seemed more interested in Jody's response than how Mia and Mutt were getting along. "What's wrong?"

"It's the first time I've seen her smile."

USA TODAY bestselling author **Alexis Morgan** has always loved reading and now spends her days imagining worlds filled with strong heroes and gutsy heroines. She is the author of over forty-five books, novellas and short stories that span a variety of romance genres. She lives in the Pacific Northwest with her husband and family.

Books by Alexis Morgan

Harlequin Heartwarming

Heroes of Dunbar Mountain

The Lawman's Promise

THE RELUCTANT GUARDIAN

ALEXIS MORGAN

LOVE INSPIRED
INSPIRATIONAL ROMANCE

LOVE INSPIRED®

INSPIRATIONAL ROMANCE

Recycling programs
for this product may
not exist in your area.

ISBN-13: 978-1-335-49845-8

The Reluctant Guardian

Love Inspired
22 Adelaide St. West, 41st Floor
Toronto, Ontario M5H 4E3, Canada
www.LoveInspired.com

Printed in U.S.A.

Lo, children are an heritage of the Lord:
and the fruit of the womb is his reward.
—*Psalms* 127:3

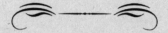

This book is dedicated to my friend Joanne.
Her friendship and support is a gift
I never take for granted.

ONE

"Stop whining, dog. Go back to bed."

Hoping Mutt would do as he was told, Conner closed his eyes and tried to drift back to sleep. The dog wasn't having it, though. He hit Conner with a blast of doggy breath and then licked his face. When that didn't work, Mutt followed it up with a soft nip on Conner's arm.

That had Conner jerking upright in the bed, knowing neither of them would get any more sleep until he figured out what his furry roommate was trying to tell him. Mutt might have reached the end of his K-9 career, but there nothing wrong with his instincts. Something wasn't right.

"Okay, I'm awake, boy."

The dog backed away and restlessly paced the floor as Conner yanked on his jeans and then shoved his feet into his shoes without bothering with socks. Not knowing what the situation was, he also grabbed the uniform shirt he'd only taken off two hours ago.

The only question was if he should take his service weapon. Erring on the side of caution, he retrieved it from the lockbox in the nightstand drawer and followed Mutt into the living room.

By that point the dog was practically vibrating as he stood by the door. "Okay, Mutt, show me."

They slipped out into the darkness without turning on the porch light. Mutt bolted past Conner and headed straight for the house next door. He had no idea what had set the dog off, but they both knew better than to go charging blindly into danger. He snapped an order, using one of the German commands Mutt had been trained to obey without question. *"Fuss!"*

Mutt immediately circled back to park himself next to Conner's left foot, content to let his human partner assess the situation. For several seconds, the normal night sounds settled around them: the rustle of leaves in the breeze, the frogs raising their usual racket in a nearby creek, the distant sound of late-night traffic out on the highway. Nothing that triggered any kind of alarm.

Then Conner finally heard what Mutt's superior hearing had picked up from inside the house— a child's scream coming from the house next door. Conner charged forward with Mutt loping along at his side. He'd only moved into his house a couple of weeks back and didn't know his neighbors at all other than to nod on the few occasions when they crossed paths. As far as he knew, the woman next door lived alone. At least he'd never seen anything that indicated there was a man or child in residence.

Not that it mattered who actually lived there—not when it sounded as if a kid was being terrorized. He circled around the low hedge that separated the two houses. At the same time, he called dispatch to alert them to the situation. No cop liked responding to a possible domestic dispute without backup. In Conner's prior job, help would've been only minutes away. In this rural county in eastern Washington, the deputies on duty might be fifty miles or more from where he stood. Even if close by, they could be caught up in their own situation, so there was no telling how soon they would head his way.

The bottom line was Conner and Mutt were on their own. The time it would take for help to arrive could be an eternity of fear and pain for a child. As if to prove his point, another scream rang out and then another. He gave the dispatcher a bare-bones description of the situation and took off running.

"Come on, Mutt. Let's go."

The dog was a silent shadow as they approached the house. Once they reached the porch, Conner edged closer to the front window, hoping to get a glimpse inside before pounding on the door. There was a light on in the hall that led out of the living room to the right. He had to guess that the floor plan of the house was the flip of his own, a small rambler with no basement. If so, that hall led to the two smaller bedrooms and a bathroom. There was a second hall to the left that led to the master bedroom, which had its own full bath. The kitchen and dining area were right behind the living room.

When another scream rang out, he banged on the front door and shouted, "Police! Open the door."

It took every ounce of strength Jody had to hold on to Mia as she strove to comfort the distraught little girl. Thank goodness the old rocker was oversize, providing ample space for the two of them. Jody guessed Mia was around three to four years old and big enough to be quite a handful when she flailed around in her distress. As a result, Jody's arms ached and her heart hurt as she continued to rock slowly back and forth, hoping Mia would find comfort in the steady rhythm and the soft murmurs of reassurance Jody offered her. The screams were getting farther apart, but that didn't matter much. Based on past experience, the little girl might be regrouping before starting up again.

Neither of them had gotten much sleep since Mia had been placed with Jody, and the stress was taking a definite toll on both of them. As she continued rocking, Jody offered up a silent prayer for strength, guidance and patience. "Honey, I know you're upset and scared, but I'm here for you."

She brushed her fingers across Mia's cheek, which was flushed red and almost fever hot from exertion. The little girl's breath came in gulps and gasps, her thin body going rigid before she started wailing again.

This time the pitiful noise ended as quickly as it started. The silence was a welcome respite. Jody drew a deep breath and let it out, doing her best to relax in case that would help calm Mia.

"I'm here for you, honey. Let's see if we can get you back to bed. I'll stay close until I know you're all right."

She muscled them both up out of the rocker. But before she could lay Mia down, someone started pounding on the front door. That set off a new round of tears from the little girl and a surge of anger from Jody. Who on earth came knocking on doors at three in the morning?

No one she was expecting, that was for sure. She crept out of the room and down the short hall to the living room, still cradling Mia in her arms.

"Police! Open the door or we're coming in!"

The police? What was going on that had brought them to her house? Then she glanced down at her small companion and knew. Someone must have heard Mia's screaming and called the authorities. Her stomach lurched. Would they revoke the placement and send the little girl to stay with some other foster family? That was the last thing Mia needed. She'd been through enough already, and another major change might be more than she could handle.

The pounding started again, leaving Jody no choice but to respond. She turned on the porch light and then retreated to an arm's length from the door. That put an end to the pounding, but not the demand. "Open up."

"Let me see your badge first."

It only took a few seconds before a badge appeared in the narrow window by the door. It was attached to a blue shirt worn by a man. Should she call 9-1-1 to verify the police were responding to a complaint at her address or simply open the door?

The badge was replaced by a man's face, one that looked vaguely familiar. Maybe if she wasn't scared half out of her wits and exhausted, she might have even recognized him before he announced, "I'm Deputy Dunne. I live next door."

Okay, that made sense. He'd only recently moved in, but she'd seen him a couple of times since the day the moving truck had come and gone. His SUV was in the driveway most mornings and gone in the evening. With everything going on in her own life, she hadn't had the time or energy to wonder if he worked nights or even what he did for a living.

"I recognize you from when you moved in."

"Are you alone, ma'am?"

She nodded. "It's just me and Mia."

His gaze flicked down toward Mia and back up. "Are you both all right?"

"Yes, we're fine." Not really, but she suspected he was concerned that one or both of them had been injured.

"I heard screaming. I need to see for myself that the little girl is okay."

She glanced down at Mia's tearstained face and wondered what the deputy would think when he saw her. Only one way to find out. "I'm going to unlock the door now."

She undid the dead bolt and quickly retreated to the other side of the room before calling out, "Come in."

The door opened slowly, giving the deputy a chance to scope out the room. His eyes went first to her and then to Mia, who stared back at him with her thumb in her mouth. He pushed the door open farther. "We're coming in. My dog is a trained police dog, and we'll be searching the house to verify you're not in any danger."

With that, an enormous German shepherd stalked into the room. The deputy quickly scanned the living room and the kitchen beyond and then patted the dog on the head as he said, *"Voran."*

She didn't know what the word meant, but the dog sure did. He immediately disappeared down the hall that led to Mia's room and the spare bedroom Jody used for an office. She could hear him sniffing his way from one room to the next. He reappeared in no time and made the same kind of excursion into Jody's bedroom and en suite bathroom. When he returned, the dog sat down next to Deputy Dunne as if awaiting new orders. If it weren't the middle of an already stressful night, Jody would've found the entire process fascinating.

"Mutt heard the girl screaming all the way from next door."

It wasn't quite an accusation, but it came pretty darn close. With her emotions feeling so raw, Jody fought for a bit of calm before responding. She couldn't afford for this cop to report back to CPS that she wasn't providing adequate care for Mia.

"She does that at night, but we're trying to work through it."

How much should she tell him? Probably more than she wanted to, but this might not be the only time Mia's distress might disturb the dog's sleep in the middle of the night. "Look, would you like a cup of tea or something? I promise I'll explain."

Without waiting for a response, she carried Mia into the kitchen and set her down at the table. "I'll get you some juice, sweetie."

Once she'd taken care of her charge, she put the kettle onto boil. By that point, the deputy was on the phone talking to someone named Sofie. After disconnecting the call, he took a seat at the kitchen table across from where Mia sat sipping her juice. Her eyes were huge as she stared first at him and then at the dog who'd taken a seat next to his owner.

When Mia smiled at the shepherd, Jody's heart did a stutter step. In the few days since Mia had come to stay with her, she hadn't smiled once. Nor had she spoken a single word. Jody might not be comfortable around big dogs, but it was clear that Mia felt differently.

"Don't take this wrong, but is he friendly? Your dog, I mean."

The deputy glanced down at his companion. "Mutt recently retired from the K-9 patrol and came to live with me. As far as I know, the only time he's spent around kids was when he used to do community events. He was always patient with them."

As if sensing they were talking about him, Mutt looked Jody straight in the eye. It was strange to feel as if she were being judged by the huge dog, but she really hoped that she passed inspection. When she offered him a tenuous smile, he left his owner to join Mia at the other end of the table, laying his huge head in her lap. That brought another smile to the little girl's face as she patted Mutt on the head and softly stroked his fur.

The deputy seemed more interested in Jody's response to the interaction than how Mia and Mutt were getting along. "What's wrong?"

Jody set a mug of tea down in front of him before taking a seat at the table. "It's the first time I've seen her smile."

He shot her a look of complete disbelief. "How is it possible you've never seen your daughter smile?"

Before she could answer, Mia scrambled down from her chair and took off down the hall to her bedroom with Mutt hot on her heels. Jody was immediately on her feet and following, with Deputy Dunne right behind her. The two adults stopped in the doorway and watched in astonishment as the little girl climbed back into bed and under the covers. Mutt turned in a circle twice and then curled up on the floor by the bed.

Jody didn't know what to do next. It was doubtful the deputy would lend her his dog, but it couldn't hurt to ask. Keeping her voice at a whisper, she leaned closer to him. "Could he maybe stay until she falls asleep?"

After a brief hesitation, he slowly nodded. "For a little while. I still need to know what's going on here."

"Thank you." She spoke louder when she looked across at Mia. "Mutt will hang out until you fall asleep. Then he has to go home and sleep in his own bed. Do you understand?"

Mia leaned over the edge of the bed to pat the dog again and then nodded.

"I'll leave the lamp on for you."

Jody was all too aware of the police officer following in her footsteps as she led the way back to the kitchen. She figured him to be a shade under six feet, about half a foot taller than she was. He also had a slight case of bed head, the blond waves flattened more on one side than the other. She felt a small surge of guilt to know he'd been jarred out of a sound sleep when Mia's screams had drawn the dog's attention. By that point, their tea was nearly cold, but he didn't seem all that interested in drinking it anyway. He'd pulled a small notebook from his shirt pocket and then patted his pocket as if looking for a pen. She fetched one from the counter and then sat back down.

"Okay, what do you need to know?"

"Start off with the basics—names, etc., for both you and the girl."

"I'm Jody Kruse."

She spelled her name and then rattled off her address and phone number. While he finished writing, she drew a slow breath. "We're calling her Mia. She came to stay with me three days ago. I'm her foster mother."

His expression turned grim. "What's her family situation?"

"I wish I could tell you, but we don't know." Jody took a sip of her tepid tea and grimaced. At least it soothed her parched throat. "She was found abandoned outside County Hospital in the middle of the night. All she had with her was a small backpack that held a few clothes and a stuffed toy. She was sitting alone on a bench near the emergency entrance."

Deputy Dunne was frowning big-time by that point. "No one saw anything?"

She shrugged. "The last I heard the police hadn't found any witnesses, but they're still looking. Evidently she was dropped off after the night crew came on shift. That helped narrow down the time frame, but that's all. From what the hospital told CPS, there's normally a steady stream of people going in and out of the place, but it turned out to be one of those rare quiet nights. If an orderly from the evening shift hadn't come back for something he'd forgotten, there's no telling how long Mia would've been out there on that bench."

How scared must she have been sitting there alone in the chilly darkness? Jody had her own experience with guardian angels protecting the innocent, and she could only be grateful that one must have been watching over Mia that night.

"I'm guessing there weren't any security cameras in the area."

"Not in that particular area, or at least that's what I was told."

"What does Mia have to say about what happened?"

"Nothing."

Dunne set his pen down, the disbelief in his icy blue eyes all too clear. "I'm not great at guessing how old a kid is, but even I know she's old enough to talk. What does she say when you ask about her parents?"

Jody found herself praying for patience for a second time that night. "Our best guess is that she's somewhere between three and four years old. So, yes, she is plenty old enough to talk. She just won't. The doctors say there's no obvious physical reason they can find for her silence, so we're pretty sure it's trauma related."

She offered him a rueful smile. "You know firsthand that her vocal cords work, but sadly the only sound she makes is when she wakes up screaming at night. The social worker and I have tried other things. If we ask her to write her name, she only scribbles. When we ask her where her family is, she draws a car. If we ask about her mother, she shakes her head. We don't know what that means. It could be she doesn't have one or that she doesn't know where she is. She gets more upset when we ask about her father."

"Any signs of abuse?"

"Not any obvious ones. No bruises, scars or anything like that. The doctor who examined her in the ER described her as well nourished, if that means anything."

"Any fingerprints on the stuff she had with her?"

"If they've learned something useful, I haven't heard about it. Maybe the tests were inconclusive."

"Anything else I should know?"

Jody shook her head. "Only that I'm sorry she woke you up, Deputy Dunne. I'm hoping the screaming will stop once she realizes she's safe with me."

"Might as well call me Conner."

The offer was said a bit grudgingly, but she took it as a sign she had gone from being a suspect to…well, she wasn't sure what exactly. Regardless, somewhere in the last few minutes, his demeanor had changed. He seemed less confrontational and more concerned.

"If you'll call me Jody." She offered him a small smile. "I appreciate that you and Mutt came running when you thought a child was in danger."

"It's my job."

That was true, but she doubted that his job description included letting his dog stand guard so a scared little girl could go back to sleep. Rather than point that out, Jody stood up. "I'll go check on Mia.

Hopefully she's settled in for the night so you and Mutt can get some sleep."

Once again, he followed after her, explaining the dog might not leave unless Conner ordered him to stand down. To Jody's relief, Mia was sound asleep, her face peaceful and relaxed. When she started toward the bed, Conner put his hand on her shoulder to stop her.

"Let me."

When he stepped around her, Mutt opened his eyes and focused all his attention on his owner. Conner softly whispered a word that sounded like "hoose." She wasn't sure what it meant, but the dog lurched to his feet and silently followed his owner out of the room and down the hall to the living room.

Before Conner opened the door, he scribbled something on a piece of paper from his notebook and held it out. "I mostly work evenings, but I can get called out anytime they need me. Here's my direct phone number. Don't hesitate to use it. You know, just in case."

She was still trying to figure out in case of what when he and Mutt disappeared into the darkness outside, pausing only to issue one last command. "Lock the door."

Jody was too tired to object to being ordered around. Instead, she did as he said before heading back to check on Mia one last time before seeking out her own bed.

TWO

Both Conner and Mutt had been too wound up to go right back to bed after leaving Jody's place. Instead, they'd enjoyed a long walk along the stream on the other side of the road. It had taken an hour to burn off the adrenaline rush before returning home. On the way back, he'd stopped to study Jody's house for a few seconds. It was a relief to see the lights were off in both the kitchen and living room. With luck, that meant the woman and the little girl were sound asleep.

He hoped so, for their sakes. Jody Kruse had looked as if it had been days since she'd gotten any rest. Her shoulder-length hair had been a messy halo of dark curls. Coupled with the circles under her brown eyes, there had been a waiflike look about her that stirred his protective instincts to life. When it had come time to leave, he'd had to fight against a powerful urge to stand guard over her the same way Mutt had done for Mia. However, his job was to assess the situation, especially regarding the little girl's safety. One way or another, he needed to remain impartial.

As a result, sleep hadn't come easily for him even after the walk. He couldn't quit thinking about Mia and wondering what kind of person would've dumped off a kid like that. Experience had taught him that sometimes desperate people did desperate things. But if there was a legitimate reason they could no longer care for Mia, why not ask for help? Granted, they'd left her outside a hospital, but that was no guarantee that she'd be found by someone who could be trusted to do the right thing. So why there? And why in the middle of the night? Without those answers, it would be impossible to know if there was danger dogging the little girl's footsteps.

Regardless, something had traumatized her to the point she either wouldn't or couldn't talk. Whatever it was had to be the reason behind those terrified screams.

It wasn't Conner's case, but he still wanted to see what he could learn about it. With that in mind, he left for work early in case he could catch the investigating detective at his desk.

Luck was with him. Although he was still getting to know the other deputies and detectives, he'd already crossed paths with Jack Galloway on another case. The detective was on the phone when Conner walked in, but he smiled and motioned for him to have a seat. After he hung up, Jack leaned back in his chair, the springs creaking loudly. He was a big guy, probably in his early fifties judging by his salt-and-pepper hair and the deep lines around his eyes and mouth.

"What can I do for you, Deputy?"

"I was wondering what you could tell me about the little girl who was found abandoned outside County Hospital."

Jack sat up straighter as he went on point. "What's your interest?"

Conner hastened to assure the man he wasn't meaning to tread on anyone's toes. "I had to go back to Seattle for a few days to testify in a trial and was out of town when she was found. As a result, I missed the whole thing, but it turns out she's fostering with the woman who lives next door to me."

"And?"

Conner didn't want to cause his neighbor any problems, so he chose his words carefully. "And I wanted to find out if there's anything I should keep an eye out for while she's staying there."

Jack eased back in his chair again, looking more relaxed. "So far we're drawing a complete blank on who she is and where she came from. If that kid has any family, they're not doing anything to find her. Her prints aren't in any database, although we keep checking. We've sent DNA samples to be tested, but it's only been a few days, and no results so far."

"And no idea where she came from at all?"

Jack's frustration was obvious. "Nope. We've checked all the cameras in the area around the hospital, but it's like looking for a needle in a haystack. Even if we did get a shot of the vehicle she was in, we might not be able to see her considering how short she is. We sent her backpack and everything in it to the lab to see what they can find, but I'm not holding out a lot of hope at this point. We've got feelers out with various agencies in the region, but no one has anything useful to say so far."

All that meshed with what Jody had told Conner, which reassured him at least a little. He felt really sorry for the kid. Mia had to be feeling lost and terrified, surrounded as she was by strangers and having no idea where her family had gone.

He and Mutt would definitely be keeping an eye on things next door. "Well, I appreciate the information. If I can do anything to help, let me know."

"Will do." Jack hesitated a second before asking, "What can you tell me about your neighbor? What's she like?"

"I don't know her at all, but she seemed nice enough. I only moved into my house a week or so ago. I've been working evenings, so I don't see much of my neighbors."

Jack reached for a file from the stack on his desk, an obvious hint that he needed to get back to work. "Got it. Thanks for letting me know that you're nearby the kid, though. Until we learn more about the situation, we're not sure what to expect."

Conner couldn't help but agree. They might not know specifics, but it was a pretty fair guess that whatever had led to Mia ending up on that bench hadn't been anything good. For now, he needed to get out on the road.

Thanks to Mutt's help getting Mia back to bed, Jody enjoyed a solid six hours of sleep herself. As a result, she'd woken up feeling more rested than she had in days. She and Mia enjoyed bowls of oatmeal for breakfast, although the little girl still seemed puzzled over why they had to wait to eat until after Jody said the blessing. Even so, she sat quietly and waited for the okay to dig in. It reminded Jody of her own experience back when she'd been placed in foster care. At least she'd been in her early teens and more capable of understanding her foster parents' explanation of what was happening.

After breakfast, she helped Mia get dressed. She'd arrived with only the bare minimum of clothing, so Jody planned to go online later and order a few more items to supplement her meager wardrobe. Meanwhile, she'd asked Mia to play in her room while Jody showered and got ready to face the day. Mia's caseworker was coming by later in the morning to check on them both, and she wanted to look her best.

It was hard not to be anxious about the upcoming visit. To keep herself busy, Jody decided to ask Mia to help her bake some muffins. It wasn't the first time she'd enlisted the little girl's help in the kitchen, figuring it was a fun way for the two of them to spend time together. Besides, offering refreshments to Mrs. Caldwell seemed like a nice thing to do. Like most people in her profession, the woman was no doubt overworked and underpaid. She also routinely dealt with kids and families that were in crisis mode. Maybe a cup of coffee and a fresh-baked muffin would provide a positive moment in the midst of all that other stuff.

"Mia, do you want to help me bake muffins for when Mrs. Caldwell comes to visit us this morning?"

The little girl dropped the crayon she'd been drawing with and scampered into the kitchen. She dragged the closest chair from the table over to the counter and climbed up next to Jody. When she tried to hand Mia a spoon, the little girl frowned and looked around the kitchen before finally pointing toward a drawer on the other side of the stove.

She hadn't done that before. "What is it you need?"

It was too much to hope that Mia would simply answer the question. Instead, she scrambled back down and headed toward the drawer. After yanking it open, she pulled out one of the large kitchen towels that were stored there. Then she did her best to wrap it around her waist like an apron. When it kept falling off, Jody helped her tie it securely.

"Good idea, Mia. We should both wear aprons."

Jody got her own out of the drawer and put it on before lifting Mia back up on the chair. At the same time, she wondered who had taught Mia about aprons and that a dish towel could be used in a pinch. "Do you always wear an apron when you cook?"

When Mia nodded, she asked another question. "Do you like to cook?"

That brought a small smile to the little girl's face. Jody debated asking a few more yes-or-no questions but decided against it for the moment. Mia was clearly excited about getting to help, and pressing for answers might ruin the experience for her. Better to enjoy the moment and hope that Mia would eventually come to trust Jody with her secrets.

She set the oven to preheat and then got out the ingredients they'd need for the muffins. When everything was arranged, she picked up a container of blueberries in one hand and a Granny Smith apple in the other. "What do you think, Mia? Would she like blueberry or apple cinnamon better?"

Mia immediately pointed toward the blueberries. Jody put the apple back in the bowl and set the container of berries down in front of Mia. "Would you like to eat a couple to make sure they'll make good muffins?"

After carefully picking out three berries, Mia popped them in her mouth. As soon as she swallowed them, she rubbed her tummy and nodded. The little rascal might not talk, but she still managed to get her opinions across.

"Okay, let's get started." Jody checked the recipe and then set a measuring cup down next to the carton of berries. Pointing to the line at the top, she said, "Fill this cup with the berries up to here. While you do that, I'll get the muffin tin ready to use and start working on the dry ingredients."

Watching Mia as she measured the berries brought back good memories of the times Jody had spent cooking with her own foster mother. She'd been sent to live with Shannon and Lyle Burks in her early teens. It hadn't been an easy transition for any of them, but Jody gave thanks every day that God had brought the couple into her life. Although the placement was originally meant to be only temporary, Jody had ended up living with them until after she graduated from college and took a job teaching here on the other side of the Cascade Mountains from where the Burks lived.

Thinking about them had her studying her own small charge. She prayed that she'd learned enough from the example they'd set to provide a good home for Mia, even if it turned out to be only a temporary refuge for her.

She smiled when Mia held up the measuring cup for Jody's inspection. "You did a great job, Mia. Exactly one cup. I see there are a few left over. Should we put them back in the fridge or eat them now?"

Mia considered the matter for all of two seconds before she carefully divided the remaining berries into two equal piles of ten berries each. She waited until Jody nodded before gathering up her share and cramming them all in her mouth at one time. Before picking up her own, Jody tapped Mia on the nose with her finger. "You look like a chipmunk who has stuffed her cheeks with a bunch of nuts."

Then she picked up half of her own allotment and ate them while Mia eyed the remaining few with undisguised greed. Jody grinned at her. "Go ahead, munchkin. You can have them. Then we'd better get these muffins mixed up and in the oven."

Thanks to her helper, Jody ended up with almost as much flour on her clothes as in the bowl, but that was fun, too. The coffee was ready and the muffins out of the oven when the front doorbell rang. "That will be Mrs. Caldwell."

With that announcement, Mia was off and running for her room. Jody was torn between going after her and answering the door. Finally, she decided to invite the caseworker in and then go see what she could do to coax Mia to come meet with the woman.

She took a deep breath and then opened the door. "Please come in. I made coffee, and Mia and I baked some blueberry muffins."

That announcement clearly pleased her guest. "I'd say you shouldn't have gone to all that bother, but the truth is I could use a jolt of caffeine about now."

As Mrs. Caldwell entered the living room, she looked around and frowned. Jody figured she was concerned that Mia wasn't anywhere to be seen. "Sorry, but she's in her bedroom. If you'll have a seat at the kitchen table, I'll go get her."

Crossing her fingers things would go smoothly, she headed down the hall to Mia's room. The only

sign that she was even in there was the small sneak-
ered foot jutting out from under the bed. Jody's heart
instantly hurt for the little girl. All things considered, it came as no surprise that she'd be terrified
of strangers. Her whole life had been turned upside
down, and nothing about her world was normal right
now.

Jody perched on the side of the bed but made no
effort to physically drag the little girl out of her hiding spot. To do something like that would destroy
the fragile bit of trust they'd managed to build over
the few days they'd been together.

"Mia, I would like it if you came out from under
the bed. You've met Mrs. Caldwell before, and she's
a nice lady. Like me, she only wants what's best for
you, and that means she needs to see that I'm taking
good care of you."

No movement. She changed tactics and tried
again. "I told her that you'd helped make the muffins. I thought you'd like to be there when she tries
one. Wouldn't that be nice? Of course, you and I will
each have one, too. How does that sound?"

The foot disappeared. Jody bit her lip, trying to
think of something else that might lure her out. But
before she could come up with a single thought,
Mia's head popped out from under the bed. She was
lying on her back, so she could look up at Jody. Then
she held up two fingers.

What was she trying to tell her? Stupid question.
"Yes, you can have two. We'll all eat one, and then

Mrs. Caldwell will want to ask each of us some questions. If you'll do your best to answer them, then you can have a second one."

Apparently they had a deal. When Mia wormed her way out from under the bed, Jody held out her hand and let Mia tug her up to her feet. "Okay, are we ready?"

With a quick nod, Mia practically dragged Jody back to the kitchen. Mrs. Caldwell smiled at them both. "I hope you don't mind, but I helped myself to a cup of coffee. I wasn't sure how long—" she glanced at Mia and back at Jody "—your hall was, and I thought it might take a while for you to get back here to the kitchen."

That was tactful. No doubt she was well aware that the kids whose care she oversaw weren't always glad to see her. "I appreciate your patience. We were negotiating how many muffins Mia gets to eat. She helped me bake them. Even measured the blueberries all by herself."

"Well, that's a big-girl thing to do." Dropping her voice to a low whisper, Mrs. Caldwell nodded her head in Jody's direction. "Did you help measure the flour, or did Jody manage to spill that much on her apron all on her own?"

Mia had climbed into the chair that was the farthest from the caseworker, but at least she managed a small smile at the woman's teasing remark. Jody took that as a sign of progress. So did Mrs. Caldwell, who smiled back at the little girl. "Now, do I really get to try one of your muffins?"

Mia glanced at Jody and then nodded. She also held up one finger and then pointed at Mrs. Caldwell and then back at herself before holding up a second finger. Jody winked at her and then translated for the other woman's benefit. "I told Mia that we would each eat one muffin. And if she does her best to answer your questions, she can have a second one."

"Well, that sounds like a fair deal. Answering questions can be hard work. Think I might get a second one if I do a good job, too?"

Jody didn't have to answer, because Mia was already nodding. So far, the meeting had been smooth sailing. She could only hope that it would continue. At least Mrs. Caldwell seemed content for everyone to enjoy their muffins before starting the question-and-answer portion of the meeting.

When they were all done, she smiled at Mia. "Okay, young lady, I only have a few questions for you. Can you tell me your name?"

Silence.

"How old are you?"

Silence and a frown, but then Mia slowly held up four fingers.

"Great, you're four years old. Can you tell me who left you on that bench at the hospital the other night?"

Mia froze, her eyes huge and scared. Jody wanted to gather her into her arms and shield her from the questions that were upsetting her. But the caseworker immediately pivoted and lobbed another easy question in the little girl's direction. "Are you happy here with Jody?"

That elicited a definite nod, which was a huge relief.

"Is there anything you'd like to tell me, Mia?"

This time she shook her head and then scrambled down out of her chair, grabbing a muffin off the plate on her way. Jody thought about stopping her, but Mrs. Caldwell stepped into the breach. "Mia, thank you for answering what you could for me. Enjoy your muffin. I hope you don't mind if I have a second one, too."

Mia edged back into the room. After setting her muffin on the seat of the chair where she'd been sitting, she picked up the plate of muffins and carried them around to offer them to Mrs. Caldwell. The woman studied them carefully before making her selection. "Wow, this one has a lot of berries in it. Thank you, Mia."

Then Mia carried the plate to Jody, who took it from her. "Thank you for playing hostess, munchkin. Why don't you take your muffin to your room and look at books? After we're done here, we can read them together."

Her good mood restored, Mia skipped out of the room and disappeared from sight. Both adults drew deep breaths and let them out slowly. Mrs. Caldwell smiled at Jody. "So how are things really going for the two of you? Is she doing better sleeping through the night?"

Not exactly. It was unlikely that anything she said would surprise the woman, not when she'd done this kind of work for close to thirty years. There probably wasn't much that would shock her, and she might even have some helpful suggestions. Full disclosure was probably the best policy.

"Last night was really rough. Mia went to bed at about eight o'clock and fell right to sleep. But she woke up about two thirty in the morning screaming again. That was the longest she'd slept at a stretch, so I was hoping she'd moved past the nightmares. Poor thing was inconsolable. I've even moved a rocker into her room, because rocking seems to help calm her down. Not that it worked all that well this time."

Needing to move, she got up to top off their coffee. "She kept screaming at the top of her lungs. It was enough to wake my next-door neighbor, and he came pounding on the door at about three o'clock. His name is Conner Dunne, and he's a deputy with the county sheriff's department."

She sat back down. "He only recently moved in. I'd seen him a couple of times, but we'd never actually met. From what he told me, Mia actually woke his dog. Mutt—that's the dog's name—is a retired police dog. He alerted Conner, and they came running. Evidently he thought it was a domestic violence situation."

"What did he say when you explained the actual circumstances?"

"He insisted on him and the dog searching the

premises. You know, to make sure there was no one else in the house. I didn't like it, but I understood why he had to do that. He had Mia's welfare at heart."

Thinking about what had come next, Jody smiled. "We all sat down here at the table while I gave Mia some juice and made herbal tea for me and Deputy Dunne. Mia actually smiled for the first time since she came here when Mutt put his head on her lap and let her pet him. After she decided to put herself back to bed, Mutt stood watch until she fell asleep. The deputy and I talked a little more about Mia's situation, and then they left. He gave me his direct number in case I need him for some reason."

Mrs. Caldwell had been taking notes, but she paused to ask, "Did he mention if he was going to file a formal report about the incident?"

"He didn't say one way or the other. I know he talked to someone named Sofie, but I got the impression she was the dispatcher or something. Will it cause problems if he did?"

"I'll check in with him to see if he has any concerns I should know about." She closed her notebook and then pulled a business card out of her purse. "I'd also like to have a therapist who specializes in children like Mia do an evaluation for us. I apologize for setting up an appointment without checking with you first, but Dr. Mayberry has a pretty full schedule. She had an unexpected opening, and I grabbed it while I had the chance. It's tomorrow at ten. If you're not available to take Mia, I can do it."

Jody studied the card. "Thanks, but I can take her."

"Okay, I think that's everything. Don't hesitate to call if you have any questions." Mrs. Caldwell stood up. "And, Jody, if it gets to be too much, let me know. This is your first placement, and it's tougher than most."

Did she think that Jody was failing Mia in some way? She hoped not, because the last thing Mia needed right now was to be uprooted again. "I appreciate your concern and your support, but we're managing. I can already see a difference in her."

"That's great. Before I go, I'll see if I can catch Deputy Dunne at home."

Jody escorted Mrs. Caldwell out, partly to be polite but also to see if Conner's vehicle was next door. It came as somewhat of a relief to see his driveway was empty. Mrs. Caldwell would catch up with him eventually, but maybe his report would be more positive if he'd had a good night's sleep before then. She could only hope.

THREE

If there was one thing Conner hated, it was being woken up from a sound sleep twice in as many days. He didn't bother putting on shoes or combing his hair before trudging to the front door with Mutt following in his footsteps. Right now, all he wanted to do was tell his unexpected visitor to get lost and then crawl back into bed. Thanks to a three-car accident out on the interstate, Conner's shift had run long by almost three hours. It was part of the job. But once he'd finally made it home, he desperately needed some uninterrupted sleep before he had to be back on duty again.

He unlocked the door and opened it. The grandmotherly woman on his porch probably didn't deserve the sharp side of his tongue, but he wasn't sure he could pull off warm and friendly right now. He settled for getting right to the point. "Can I help you?"

She held out a business card. "I'm Margie Caldwell. I work for CPS here in the county."

He squinted down at the tiny print. "You're here about the little girl next door."

"Yes, I am. I apologize for disturbing you, but Ms. Kruse told me you responded to an incident night before last. I was wondering if we could talk about it."

He glanced toward Jody's place and wondered if she knew about this. Not his problem. The caseworker's focus had to be on the welfare of the child, so he would do his best to answer her questions. Stepping back, he invited her in. "Come on in and have a seat. I'll be back in a minute."

Then he stopped. "I'm guessing you already know I have a dog. Mutt is a retired K-9 dog and well-mannered. He won't bother you, but I'll put him out in the backyard."

She took a seat on the couch while the German shepherd quietly watched her from across the room. Conner waited until she was settled and then said, "Mutt, with me."

He turned the dog out to explore the yard and then took a minute to comb his unruly hair and brush his teeth. After putting on a sweatshirt and some socks, Conner felt slightly more civilized as he rejoined his guest.

"Sorry to keep you waiting. It was a late night on the job."

She offered him an apologetic smile. "Not a problem. I would've called first, but I neglected to ask Ms. Kruse for your number when I told her I'd be checking in with you."

The woman could have also left a message at the station that she wanted to talk to him, but he didn't bother pointing that out. Maybe she wanted to meet him away from official channels for some reason. "You've got questions."

The woman got right to the point. "Jody said you heard Mia's screams and responded as if it were a domestic violence case."

"I did. To be honest, Mutt heard her first. I didn't know what kind of situation I was walking into, so I called dispatch in case I needed backup." He ran his fingers through his hair. "I'm new to the area and hadn't met any of the neighbors yet. I wasn't sure who all lived next door."

"That's what Jody told me. She said she explained the situation with Mia. How did the little girl seem when you saw her?"

"She'd clearly been crying, but she didn't act at all afraid of Ms. Kruse, if that's what you're really asking. She was also fascinated with Mutt. He's a big dog, and lots of people find him intimidating. Not Mia, though. They took to each other immediately. After she returned to her bed, Mutt appointed himself to guard her until she went to sleep. I checked in on her again before Mutt and I went back home. I also gave my number to Ms. Kruse in case she needed anything. I haven't talked to her or Mia since."

"Did Mia talk in front of you at all?"

"Nope, not a word." He frowned. "I was under

the impression that she hasn't spoken since she was found in front of the hospital."

The caseworker sighed. "She hasn't as far as I know. I was kind of hoping maybe she might have said something to the dog."

That struck Conner as a bit funny. "I could ask him, but I'm not sure he'd be able to repeat what she said even if she had."

Mrs. Caldwell huffed a small laugh. "True enough, but I'm grasping at straws at this point. It's hard to help her when we have no idea what actually happened. I plan to check in with Detective Galloway later this afternoon. He's good about keeping me in the loop, but I like to keep on top of things."

Conner thought about telling her what he and Galloway had discussed the day before, but it wasn't his case. He'd leave it up to the detective to share what little information he had at this point. He didn't mean to be rude, but there didn't seem to be much else he could tell her. "Is that everything?"

"One last question. Did you make a formal report about the other night?"

"No, but I did talk to Detective Galloway yesterday. I thought he should know Mia is living next door to me in case something comes up."

"Okay, then. Well, I'll get going. Thank you for your time, Deputy."

He followed the caseworker back outside. Jody had just pulled into her driveway and was in the process of helping Mia out of the back seat. Jody looked a bit distracted, but she waved. He nodded to acknowledge her greeting before ducking back into the house. Standing at the edge of his living room window, he watched as Mrs. Caldwell walked over to chat with her. Their conversation didn't last long but seemed friendly enough. A couple of minutes later, Jody led Mia into their house as the caseworker drove off.

Conner let Mutt back inside and considered his options. He really should take Mutt for a run but found himself hesitating. He'd never lived next door to someone whom he'd had to deal with in his professional capacity. Would it make any future encounters awkward? He hoped not. Jody seemed like a nice woman, and little Mia was a real cutie. Conner couldn't avoid them forever. Besides, Mutt needed to burn off some energy.

He'd always figured he might have had better people skills if he hadn't spent most of his childhood living with his curmudgeon of a grandfather. He glanced at a framed photograph of him and Jasper Dunne that had pride of place on the mantel. It had been taken the night Conner graduated from high school. His grandfather had been so proud that Conner had graduated second in his class. The memory had Conner grinning. The man hadn't been the most demonstrative of people, but he'd sure stepped up to the plate when Conner had needed him. An accident involving a drunk driver had cost Conner both of his parents when he was ten. Jasper had put his own grief on hold to take charge of a boy whose life had crashed and burned.

Over the years, Jasper had shown up for baseball games and parent-teacher conferences. He'd also taken Conner to church on Sundays, because he'd known faith had been an important part of his son and daughter-in-law's lives. Jasper had quit attending services after his wife's death, but he'd found his way back to God for the sake of his grandson.

It had mostly been the two of them, but the old man had made sure Conner knew that he mattered. A master carpenter, Jasper had taught Conner to take pride in his work and to give one hundred percent to any endeavor he took on. They'd also camped and fished together. They might not have been big talkers, but they'd understood each other at a gut level. There wasn't a day that went by that Conner didn't miss the old man and hoped that he had made his grandfather proud.

After putting on his running shoes and grabbing his keys, he called Mutt in from the backyard. "Come on, dog, let's go pound the pavement."

Outside, Mutt gave the front yard a quick inspection while Conner did a few stretches. When he was ready, he clipped a long leash on Mutt's harness and started down the driveway to the street at a slow jog. They'd only gone a short distance when Mutt came to a sudden stop in front of Jody's house, his tail wagging slowly. What had caught his attention? It didn't take Conner long to figure it out. Mia was standing on the sofa that backed up to Jody's front window.

She wore a determined expression on her face as she patted her hand on the glass to get their attention. A second later, Jody appeared beside Mia when Conner waved to acknowledge her greeting. She said something to the little girl, who waved one last time before disappearing from sight. Jody stared at him briefly before turning away. He was pretty sure she'd smiled, but there was no way to know if it had been directed toward him, Mia or maybe even Mutt.

The dog continued to stare at the window as if hoping Mia would reappear. Mutt's reaction to the little girl was a bit puzzling. He was clearly taken with her for some reason, but it wasn't as if the dog had ever spent much time around little kids. His K-9 training had started when he was about eighteen months old, and he'd worked with Justin, his handler, for the better part of seven years. Mutt had also lived with Justin, who had been single.

Sadly, when it came time for Mutt to retire, Justin hadn't been able to keep him. His elderly parents had developed some serious health issues, and Justin had to leave the state to help care for them. Between them and his new job, he had all that he could handle. It had almost killed him to admit he couldn't keep Mutt.

Conner and Justin had worked together in Seattle and had become friends. They'd both enjoyed camping and hiking, and Mutt accompanied them on their outings. When Justin had to make several trips down to Arizona to check on his folks, Mutt had stayed with Conner. Upon learning Justin was going to move closer to his folks permanently, Conner offered to adopt Mutt, since the dog already knew him. The rest was history.

It took a couple of hard tugs on the leash to get Mutt moving again, but then they both got lost in the soothing rhythm of the run. Maybe if Jody was outside when they circled back toward home, he'd stop to check on Mia. Just like the caseworker, he felt a duty to make sure she was getting the best care possible. The sad fact was that some foster parents didn't always have their young charges' best interest at heart.

For everyone's sake, he really hoped Jody Kruse was one of the good guys. Mia's life might depend on it. With that unsettling thought, he kicked it into a higher gear.

Jody slipped back over to the window to watch Conner Dunne and Mutt as they ran on down the street, both man and dog moving with powerful grace. She wouldn't have noticed them passing by at all if it hadn't been for Mia. The sound of her smacking her hand on the front window was what had caught Jody's attention. Mutt had immediately stopped to acknowledge the little girl's greeting, his ears pricked forward and his tail wagging.

His owner's response was more reserved, but at least he'd waved at Mia. Jody thought he looked a bit uneasy, maybe because they'd all met under such un-usual circumstances. The man had only been doing his job, and Mrs. Caldwell had assured her that Con-ner's description of the events had matched Jody's.

In fact, most of their discussion out in the drive-way had been about Mia's appointment with the counselor. While Dr. Mayberry had been friendly, she hadn't had any better luck with getting Mia to talk. She'd hastened to tell Jody that it took time to build any kind of rapport with children who had been traumatized. She had also spent a good part of the appointment talking to Jody while Mia looked at books out in the reception area. Dr. Mayberry made a few suggestions about things to try and assured Jody she was doing a good job.

It helped to hear that. Jody was doing the best she could, but it was hard not to think she was failing Mia somehow. They were no closer to learning the truth about what had happened to Mia's family. If she really was establishing a connection with the little girl, why wouldn't Mia tell Jody what she knew? At four years of age, she should be able to explain what had happened. Even a child's description of the facts could give the police a place to start.

At the therapist's suggestion, Jody had encour-aged Mia to draw pictures to display on the refriger-ator. Dr. Mayberry had cautioned her against trying to direct the choice of subject matter and instead let-ting Mia choose what to draw. Eventually, she might reveal something that would be useful. So far, she'd done several different drawings of a large animal. The liberal use of black and tan made it clear that Mia was doing portraits of Mutt.

In one, the dog was standing next to a tall man with a yellow circle on his chest. When Jody had asked if that was a badge, Mia had given an emphatic nod and pointed toward the house next door. In another picture, the dog towered over a little girl who had light brown hair like Mia's.

"You're quite the artist, Mia. Do you want to hang a picture of Mutt on the fridge?"

Evidently the answer was yes, because she was instantly up and running toward the kitchen. Jody had already dug out a set of magnets to make it easier for Mia to manage the makeshift art gallery herself. When she had the picture arranged to her satisfaction, they both stood back to admire her artwork.

"That's beautiful, Mia. I love it." She pointed back to the other drawing. "Do you want to hang up that one, too?"

Mia shook her head and then pointed in the direction of Conner's house. "You want to give it to Mutt?"

Another nod.

"I'm not sure when we'll see him again. Why don't we keep it on the table by the front door for now? That way it will be handy if we happen to see him or Deputy Dunne when we're outside."

Mia ran back to the living room. After setting the picture on the table, she climbed back up on the couch to look out the window. Jody waited a short time before trying to distract her. "There's no telling how long they'll be gone, Mia. Let's go work out in the yard for a while. We could both use some fresh air."

There was no response for several seconds. Looking disappointed, Mia finally followed Jody into the garage to gather up their tools and a bucket. "Let's go take care of some weeds. Afterward, you can pick a bouquet of flowers to put on the kitchen table."

It didn't take long for Mia to lose interest in weeding, but she seemed content to wander around the yard checking out all the different kinds of flowers. Right now almost everything was in full bloom. Jody loved the bright splashes of colors that perennials and annuals offered. She planted a few new varieties every year, some in the ground and others in pots and hanging baskets.

She started in the far back corner digging out weeds and deadheading the roses. Along the way, she noticed that two of her new plants had been squashed flat, their stems bent and wilted. It almost looked as if someone had stepped on them at some point. Who would've done that? She'd left Mia outside for a few minutes the day before while she'd ducked back into the kitchen to get them cold drinks. Maybe the little girl had wandered into the flower bed then. If it happened again, she'd have to remind her to be more careful.

Deciding she'd done enough work for one day, she stood up and stretched. As she did, she glanced

out toward the woods located a short distance behind her back fence to see if there were any deer in
sight. She was sure Mia would get a kick out of seeing them. Those trees were one of the main reasons
she'd bought this particular house. The view of a
permanent greenbelt sure beat staring at the back of
someone else's house. Had Conner chosen his house
for the same reason?

Not that it was any of her business.

It was time to think about making some lunch for
the two of them. After gathering up her tools, she
looked around for Mia. Only a minute ago, she'd
been studying the petunias and marigolds in one of
the big flowerpots on the patio. Where had she gone?

It took a second to spot her wedged behind two
of the big rhododendrons against the fence. She was
standing on her toes and looking through a knothole into Conner's yard. Once again, the little girl
started hitting the fence with her hand, no doubt trying to get Mutt's attention. Before Jody could stop
her from bothering Conner and Mutt, the dog came
flying over the fence.

Mia was happy. Mutt was happy. But when Jody's
back gate slammed open thirty seconds later, it was
clear that Deputy Dunne wasn't.

FOUR

Conner skidded to a halt as soon as he entered Jody's backyard and did his best to look far calmer than he felt. From the wide-eyed look on Mia's face, his efforts failed miserably. When the gate slammed shut behind him, she immediately took cover behind Mutt. Jody came charging across the yard. He wasn't sure what she planned to do, but even he knew never to get between a mama bear and her cub. Jody probably wouldn't appreciate the analogy, but she looked awfully fierce.

He remained where he was and debated how best to handle the situation. He didn't want to scare Mia, but he also couldn't tolerate Mutt taking off without permission. His behavior around the little girl was unprecedented, so Conner was at a bit of a loss. Finally, he slowly approached the dog and his little friend.

Kneeling down to her level, he spoke as calmly as he could. "Mia, I didn't mean to scare you, but I was a little upset with Mutt for taking off like that. He's supposed to stay in our yard unless I give him permission to come visit you. It's not safe for him to run away, and it worried me. I wasn't sure if he wanted to play or if he sensed something was wrong. Do you understand why that's a problem for me?"

She frowned and cocked her head to one side to study him as she considered his explanation. At the same time, she stroked Mutt's back. It was hard to tell if she was drawing comfort from touching the dog or offering him her reassurance that all was well. Finally, she slowly nodded and stepped away from Mutt to head straight for Jody. The dog watched her progress but made no move to follow.

Conner rose to his feet and gave Mutt a stern look. Pointing to the ground, he said, *"Platz."*

When the dog immediately lay down as instructed, Conner patted him on the head to let him know that all was forgiven. "Stay there, Mutt."

He'd made peace with Mia and forgiven Mutt. Now came the hard part—facing off against the mama bear. While he'd been dealing with the dog, Jody had opened the back door to let the little girl go inside. It was probably better that way. Mia didn't need to hear the two adults arguing if their discussion turned hot.

Rather than giving Jody a chance to tear into him, he started talking first and fast. "I'm sorry if I scared Mia, but she's got to learn that Mutt isn't an ordinary dog. He isn't a danger to either of you, but he can be to other people when the occasion calls for it. Thanks to his training, his job is to work with a human partner. That's why it's imperative for him to follow the rules and listen to my orders. My best guess is that for whatever reason, he's decided that Mia is a puppy that needs looking after."

When Jody started to interrupt, he cut her off. "I'm not saying that's a bad thing. What I am saying is that he's acting out of character for him. As his owner, it's my job to make sure that he follows the rules. Jumping over the fence without permission is definitely not okay. He's not the typical family pet. If Mia wants to visit with Mutt, she needs to ask permission first, and it will have to be under supervision."

He paused for effect and added, "Meaning *my* supervision. Even then, I'm not sure it's a good idea."

Jody glanced toward the house and then back at him, her face set in angry lines. "And considering she's still not talking, how is she supposed to ask?"

Right. That was a problem. "So, what do you suggest? You seem to have no trouble understanding what she wants."

"I'll try to explain the situation. I'm not sure how much she'll understand." She bit her lower lip as she gave the matter some thought. "Maybe if there's a day when you're going to be around, we could schedule something. It wouldn't have to be a long visit."

All things considered, his life would be a lot simpler if he made a clean break of it and said that there should be no further interaction between Mia and the dog. Unfortunately, it would take a much harder man than he was to do that. According to Jody, meeting Mutt the other night had been the first time the little girl had smiled. If spending a little time with the dog helped her even a little, so be it.

"I work evenings, so it will have to be in the morning. Since she's already seen him today, let's schedule it for ten o'clock day after tomorrow." So she'd know he wasn't trying to put them off, he added, "He has an appointment with the vet tomorrow morning, so we won't be around before I have to leave for work. Will that work for you?"

It occurred to him that he didn't know what Jody did for a living. It was unlikely that she could support herself and the little girl on the stipend the state paid for foster care.

"If mornings won't work because of your job schedule, we'll have to set a time on my next day off."

She shook her head and smiled. "I teach third grade at the local elementary school, so I'm off for summer vacation. If Mia is still living with me when school starts, I'll have to see about finding daycare for her."

It was impossible to miss the sadness in her voice when she mentioned the possibility of Mia being back with her family. In an ideal world, that would be a good thing. But cops and foster parents knew firsthand this world was far from perfect. That Mia had been left for strangers to find was clearly an act of desperation. It was hard to imagine a happy outcome.

The smart thing for Jody to do was take care of

the little girl without getting too attached, but it was obviously too late for that. Both woman and child would be in for a rough time when it came time for Mia to leave. Honestly, he'd miss her, too. Something about that little girl's big eyes really tugged at his heartstrings.

Especially because he remembered how hard it was to lose your entire family overnight. He'd been lucky to have his grandfather. Even if Mia had no blood relatives, at least she would have Jody.

Speaking of the little rascal, she came darting back outside with a piece of paper clutched in her hand. She gave Jody a questioning look and pointed toward him. Jody smiled and nodded. "I'm sure Deputy Dunne will love it, Mia."

He wanted to ask what he was going to love, but Mia was already headed straight for him. She stopped just shy of where he stood, close enough that she had to tip her head back to look up at him. Looking a little nervous, she held out the paper. When he accepted her offering, she retreated a few steps and watched him with a hopeful look on her face.

He studied the crayon creation for a few seconds. He was no connoisseur of toddler artwork, but even he could tell it was a picture of him and Mutt.

"Mia, this is amazing. I can tell you worked really hard on this. Mutt looks handsome, and I look… well, I look like me. I especially like how my badge is all bright and shiny. Thank you."

He might have kept right on babbling, but Mia

grabbed his hand. She led him toward Jody's back door and pointed inside. He leaned in closer to the glass slider to see what she wanted him to look at in the kitchen. It didn't take long to spot the piece of paper stuck on the front of the refrigerator. Judging from the colors and general shape, he had to guess it was another portrait of Mutt.

"It looks exactly like him, Mia. You're quite the artist." He gently ruffled her hair. "I'm guessing I'm supposed to hang this in a place of honor on my own refrigerator."

Both Mia and Jody nodded. "You used magnets, but I'm not sure I have any. Would tape be okay?"

That earned him another emphatic nod. "Okay, then. Now Mutt and I need to go back home."

When Mia immediately started toward the dog, Jody called her back. "Wait here, sweetie. Officer Dunne said we have to wait for Mutt to be told it's okay. That's really important for us to remember if you want to get to visit Mutt sometimes."

That edict didn't go over well, but Mia remained at Jody's side while Conner walked back to where Mutt lay watching them. When Conner reached the dog, he praised him for following orders. "Good boy, Mutt. Now, go say goodbye to Mia before we go back home. I need to get ready for work."

It was never clear how many words the dog actually understood outside of the German-language commands that had been part of his police training, but he obviously recognized Mia's name. Mutt and his little friend started for each other, meeting in the middle of the yard while Conner and Jody both kept a wary eye on their interaction. Mia gently wrapped her little arms around Mutt's neck and rested her head against his neck. The embrace lasted only a few seconds before Mia stepped back and patted the big dog's head. He rewarded her with a slurp of his tongue across her cheek, which left her giggling.

Jody's gaze met Conner's, her dark eyes bright with a sheen of tears although she was smiling. He understood her reaction to the little girl's unabashed happiness. He tried not to feel guilty for separating the pair, but he really did need to get a move on.

"I'm sorry, Mia, but Mutt has to go home now. I have to change into my uniform and report in at the police station."

She frowned and pointed to the picture she'd drawn him. "That's right. I have to put on my badge and drive around in my cruiser. I won't get back home until way after you have gone to bed for the night."

He hated the flash of fear that crossed her face. "Jody will keep you safe, Mia. And if she needs help, she can call me. No one is going to bother you with the two of us watching over you."

She responded by pointing at Mutt and holding up three fingers. "Sorry, you're right. I should've said no one will bother with the three of us watching over you."

Jody followed him to the gate. "I appreciate your patience with her."

He let Mutt walk out ahead of him. "We'll see you day after tomorrow. Say, around ten?"

"That will be fine, but I won't tell Mia ahead of time. I'm not sure how well she'd handle the disappointment if something comes up, and you can't make it. I'm sure a police officer's schedule isn't always predictable."

It bothered him how glad he was that she didn't think he'd blow them off for no good reason. Regardless, it was definitely past time for him to get back over to his own place before he forgot that keeping a big-eyed little girl and her pretty foster mother safe was anything more than part of his job.

Things had been quiet since Conner had retrieved Mutt the day before yesterday. Whenever she and Mia left the house for any reason, the little girl had looked longingly at the house next door in the hope that her four-legged friend would come bounding outside to see her. Clearly she was totally smitten with Mutt, making Jody wonder if there been a dog in her life before she'd come to stay with her.

Right now, the two of them were putting the finishing touches on some sugar cookies. Jody had done the heavy lifting when it came to making them, but Mia was responsible for the decorations. To say her designs were somewhat whimsical was putting it mildly. She hoped that Conner would eat them no matter how they looked. They were to be his reward for letting Mia play with Mutt. It wouldn't have come as a surprise if he'd found some excuse to cancel, but he hadn't so far.

"You did a great job on that one, Mia. I like the mix of sprinkles you used."

She let her add a few more finishing—if messy—touches to the rest of the cookies. When Mia was done, Jody brought out a large paper plate. "Now, pick a dozen of your favorites—that's twelve—for Deputy Dunne and arrange them on this plate."

While Mia selected the cookies, Jody held up the organic dog snacks she'd picked up at the pet store. Pointing at a second plate, she asked, "Should we put these on same plate as the sugar cookies or should Mutt get his own?"

Mia immediately reached for the plate and spent far more time arranging Mutt's treats than she had the cookies. Would Conner be jealous or would he be amused to learn his position in the hierarchy? There was no way to know.

Maybe she'd ask him. Meanwhile, she finished cleaning up the kitchen. After putting away the last few ingredients, she checked the time. If she hurried, she could squeeze in a quick call to Mrs. Caldwell to see about scheduling Mia's next appointment with Dr. Mayberry. It wasn't unusual that the call went to voice mail. However, this time the recording said that Mrs. Caldwell was unavailable and that all calls should be directed to Dale Greve, her supervisor.

Funny that Mrs. Caldwell hadn't mentioned anything about taking time off work, but people couldn't exactly schedule when they'd get sick or when a family emergency might pop up. She dialed Mr. Greve's number and waited for him to answer.

"Dale Greve speaking. Hold, please."

The line went silent before Jody could respond. When it stayed that way for more than four minutes, she almost hung up. Luckily, Mr. Greve finally came back on the line. "Sorry about that, but things are a little hectic around here. How can I help you?"

She suspected that things were always a little hectic there, but something in his voice made her think that he meant it was worse than usual.

"This is Jody Kruse. I tried calling Mrs. Caldwell to see if she's scheduled another appointment for Mia with Dr. Mayberry. The message said to call you instead."

He didn't immediately respond. Finally, he sighed. "I take it you haven't heard."

His words set her pulse to racing. Whatever put that dark note in his voice couldn't be good. "About what, Mr. Greve?"

Again, another hesitation. "I'm sorry to say that Mrs. Caldwell was the victim of a vicious attack two days ago right outside her home."

Had the temperature in the kitchen just dropped twenty degrees? "Is she all right?"

"She's in the hospital, but I'm not at liberty to share the details about her injuries."

That was understandable. "Do the police know who did it or why?"

"No arrests have been made to my knowledge. We don't know if it was a random mugging or if she was deliberately targeted. The authorities are still waiting to talk to her, so they don't have much to go on. We do know that her purse and briefcase were both taken, so it might be a mugging gone wrong."

Jody pulled out a kitchen chair and sat down. "Or it could be someone trying to track down one of Mrs. Caldwell's clients."

After a slight hesitation, he said, "We don't know that."

Which was another way of saying that it was a possibility. "And you said this happened two days ago?"

"Yes, evidently she'd stopped back by her house. I believe it was around eleven thirty when the neighbor found her and called the police. We figured she was going to eat lunch and make calls from home. She did that sometimes."

All this was adding up to be pretty scary. "Mr. Greve, I saw Mrs. Caldwell just before that. She stopped by to talk to my neighbor, Deputy Conner Dunne. After that, she and I talked about how Mia's first session with Dr. Mayberry had gone. She was going to schedule a second appointment and get back to me."

"At the police's request, we've been trying to reconstruct her appointment schedule for that day but haven't gotten very far with it. I will have to let the detective know that she'd been by your house. That may have been her last stop before she went home."

Jody glanced toward the living room where Mia had settled in to color while they waited for Conner and Mutt to arrive. "Should I be concerned?"

"Let's see what the police have to say, Ms. Kruse. As I said, at this point we have no reason to believe that this was anything but a random mugging. If that changes, I will make sure the police notify you."

She fought to sound far more calm than she felt. "I would appreciate it, Mr. Greve. And if you talk to Mrs. Caldwell, tell her I'll be praying for her."

"I will. I will also schedule that appointment with Dr. Mayberry and get back with you."

"Thank you."

Then she hung up and did exactly what she promised to do—she prayed for Mrs. Caldwell's quick recovery. And while she was at it, she asked God to watch over Mia as well. She also needed to tell Conner what she'd learned about Mrs. Caldwell, but it would have to wait until she had him alone.

A movement outside the front window caught her attention. "Well, little one, look who's come to visit."

As soon as Mia spotted Conner, she was off and running for the front door. She had it open before Jody even had time to take off her apron. Conner hovered in the doorway, evidently waiting for her to issue an official invitation to enter.

"Come on in, Deputy."

He shot her a quick look. "'Deputy' sounds a bit formal, don't you think?"

Yeah, it probably did, so she tried again. "Would you like to come in, Conner?"

He grinned a little. "I was thinking maybe Mia and I could take Mutt for a walk. I saw a park a few blocks away and thought she might like to play on the climber. You're welcome to come, too, if you'd like."

Why not?

"We'd like that, wouldn't we, sweetie?"

An emphatic nod left no doubt about Mia's opinion, but she held out her hand to Conner and led him over to the kitchen. Jody wished she could snap a picture of his expression as he stared down at the cookies slathered with globs of icing and random clusters of sprinkles and colored sugar. "Are these for me?"

Jody struggled not to laugh at the half-hopeful tone in his voice when he asked the question. "I baked the cookies, but Mia decorated them. I tested one out, and they were delicious."

Then she winked at him and whispered, "And safe to eat. Scout's honor."

When he picked one up and started to take a bite, Mia yanked on his arm and shook her head. Puzzled, he set it back down on the plate. "Am I eating the wrong one? Do you want to choose one for me?"

She shook her head and then put her palms together and bowed her head. He looked puzzled and then quickly nodded. "You want me to say grace first."

Mia's smile appeared to be all the answer he needed. He put his much bigger hands together and bowed his head. "We thank You, Lord, for the food before us. Amen."

Mia's head popped back up, and she offered him the cookie he'd originally picked. "Thank you, Mia."

She set that plate back down and reached for Mutt's. Conner interceded before Jody could say anything. "He can only have one, Mia. He's a bit of a pig when it comes to doggy treats. Before you give it to him, hold your hand up like this."

He turned his back to the dog and demonstrated what he meant by holding out his arm with his hand bent up with the tips of his fingers touching each other. "Now, you do it."

Mia mimicked Conner's signal, her little face scrunched up in concentration. Mutt immediately sat down, his attention never wavering from the cookie clutched in Mia's hand. She looked so proud when he carefully accepted the treat.

"Good job, kiddo. I'll let you give him another one if he behaves while we're on our walk."

Turning his attention back in her direction, he asked, "Jody, is there anything we need to take with us or are we ready to go?"

She appreciated him asking. "Let me grab some drinks to take with us. I'm guessing playing on a climber and walking Mutt will be thirsty work. It will only take a minute."

"No problem. We'll wait out front."

As she dug out a small insulated bag to hold the drinks, she replayed the last few minutes in her head.

There were a lot of ways Conner could've reacted to Mia's insistence that he say grace before eating a cookie. Some people might have laughed it off or ignored her request altogether. Instead, he hadn't hesitated to offer up the simple prayer. The man was simply full of surprises.

FIVE

Because of Mia's excitement, it took Conner a while to pick up on Jody's tension, but she didn't seem inclined to fill him in on what was wrong. Eventually, he'd probably have to pry it out of her. Meanwhile, Mutt circled around the climber keeping an eye on Mia as she clambered up one side and down the other of the large wooden structure. Conner found it amusing when Jody called a halt to Mia's playing long enough to explain that the only acceptable technique for using the slide was to sit on her backside and go down. Clearly, there were rules about such things.

He'd waited until Mia was off and running again to sidle up to Jody. "So when did it become illegal to go up a slide?"

She gave him one those looks that clearly said "respect my rules." But then she sighed. "Fine. There's a similar climber at the grade school where I work. When you have a whole lot of kids playing on it at the same time, it's total chaos without some rules in place."

She stopped to issue another edict. "Use both hands on the ladder, Mia."

He laughed. "I need to jot down all of these rules and regulations in case I ever get assigned to direct toddler traffic on a climber someday."

Her expression made it clear that he wasn't as funny as he thought he was. "I'll have you know that playground safety is a major concern in elementary schools. Sometimes there are only few adults watching a hundred-plus kids at recess."

Okay, that image made him shudder. That was a ton of responsibility to shoulder on a daily basis. "I can see how tough that would be."

Speaking of keeping a kid safe, Jody continued to scan the area in between bouts of enforcing climber safety. Was she concerned about something specific or just being extra careful since they were out in public? Looking around, there were a few parents with their kids, a group of women power walking along the trail that circled the park and a pair of older men studying a chessboard at a nearby picnic table.

Nothing unusual, but Jody wasn't the only one whose spidey senses were going off. Mutt had suddenly turned his back on Mia and stood staring off into the distance. His ears were pricked forward, his tail still as he watched…what?

There wasn't anything that set off obvious alarms, but Conner trusted the dog's instincts. Maybe it was time to stretch his legs and do a circuit around the immediate area. "Jody, I'd like to give Mutt a quick walk before it's time to head back home. We won't be out of sight. Give a shout if you need us."

Despite his best efforts to keep it casual, Jody frowned. "Is something wrong? Should we leave?"

While he didn't want to scare Jody, he also needed her to trust him. "I'm not sure. Mutt is concerned about something, and I want to see what it is."

He glanced at the dog, who had his attention laser focused on something in the parking lot.

Jody relaxed, at least a little. "We'll be here. In fact, I'll corral Mia and have her drink her juice. You probably need to be getting back anyway."

"Not quite yet, but soon."

He clipped on Mutt's leash. "Come on, boy. Let's check things out."

The dog gave Mia one last look before falling into step with Conner. They maintained a steady pace along the paved path that crisscrossed the park, slowing down when they reached the edge of the parking lot. Mutt stopped to sniff the ground, swinging his head from side to side.

Regrettably, it was impossible to tell if the scent the dog found fascinating was due to a raccoon recently passing through the area or if it was a human who presented a threat of some kind. As the dog finished his examination of that particular patch of grass, Conner did a slow turn to see if he could pick up on anything that would explain the dog's earlier reaction or his own uneasy feelings.

Nothing. There was no one lurking at the edge of

the woods that bordered the other side of the parking lot or sitting in their car watching the kids playing in the park. One car was just leaving, but there wasn't anything particularly suspicious about that. After another few seconds, he gave up. "Come on, dog. Let's head back home. I need to get ready for work."

Mutt was only too happy to return to Mia, who was finishing off her juice when they walked up. Jody took the empty box and put it back into the bag she'd brought to the park.

Despite not having found anything suspicious, Conner would feel better when Mia and Jody were safely back home. "Are you guys ready to head out?"

Mia nodded and put her hand on Mutt's harness in preparation. She walked with him while Jody walked beside Conner. Sharing the moment with the silent child and her caretaker seemed almost surreal to him. He had friends, of course. Some of them were even married with families, but he rarely spent much time around their wives and kids.

"You're thinking pretty hard there, Deputy Dunne."

Her smile made it clear that she'd used his title deliberately, maybe her way of asking if everything was okay without alarming Mia. "I was trying to figure out how long it's been since I was on an outing like this."

"And?"

"Maybe never."

He hoped that didn't sound as pathetic to her as it did to him, but then she gave him an easy out. "I imagine police officers all work long hours. It must make it difficult to have much of a social life, especially if you're always working evenings or nights."

"True, not to mention all too often the women I meet aren't very happy to have a cop show up on their doorstep."

Thanks to the other night, he knew she had her own experience with exactly how that felt. At least Jody didn't seem to hold it against him. By that point, they were almost back home. As usual, the neighborhood was quiet. A few people were working in the yard, and the mail carrier was making his rounds. Nothing out of the ordinary, but he still couldn't shake the feeling that he'd missed identifying a threat back at the park.

Mia continued to focus all her attention on Mutt, who seemed relaxed at the moment. Evidently whatever had bothered him at the park hadn't followed them home. Even so, Conner wasn't surprised when Jody once again circled back to the situation at the playground.

"Were you able to figure out what had Mutt so worried earlier?"

Conner stopped briefly to do a 360-degree turn. He couldn't pinpoint the cause of his unease, and Mutt didn't seem concerned about anything.

Running his fingers through his hair, Conner sighed. "No, which is frustrating. I'd like to say it was nothing, but I can't swear that's true. Something back there definitely bothered Mutt."

"Does that mean we should stay away from the park?"

It was time to get some answers. "That all depends on what has you so worried."

She blinked as if his assessment of her current mood surprised her. When she finally answered, she spoke in a low whisper. "I found out just before you came that Mrs. Caldwell was assaulted outside her home two days ago. It happened right after she talked to you about the night Mia woke you up. All of her calls are being referred to her supervisor. From what he said, the police don't have much to go on. He thought they might want to talk to me when I said she'd been at my house shortly before the attack."

All that came out in a rush, her dark eyes wide with worry. Conner asked the obvious question. "Do they have any idea about motive?"

"They thought it might be a robbery gone wrong." She visibly shivered. "She has a lot of clients, but I can't help but worry that this has something to do with Mia. So back to my question. Should I keep her out of sight?"

It was tempting to say yes, that Mia needed to stay home as much as possible. But without something more concrete to go on, that wouldn't be fair to Mia and would only scare Jody. He settled for offering the best advice he could.

"I wouldn't go that far quite yet, but it's always better to be proactive when it comes to keeping kids safe. That's especially true when it comes to ones like Mia where we don't know what kind of danger she might be in, if any. Use your common sense. I'll also see if I can track down the detective who is handling the case to see what they think."

That last part seemed to be the reassurance Jody needed. At any rate, she looked a little less worried. By that point, they'd reached her driveway. She paused to give Mutt a careful pat on his head. "If you two will wait here, Mia and I will go get your cookies. I wouldn't want you to miss out on all that sugary goodness. In case you're wondering, I didn't make the treats for Mutt. I bought them at the pet store in town. They're supposed to be organic and good for dogs."

He laughed. "If they're that healthy, maybe I should trade with him. He'd probably like all of those sprinkles."

Jody arched an eyebrow and gave him a narrow-eyed look. "You'd do that after all the hard work Mia put into fancying up those cookies just for you?"

She was right. There was no way he could disappoint the little girl. "Fine. I'll take a sugar-laden hit for the team."

He and Mutt waited at the end of the driveway until Jody returned with the two paper plates. She let Mia offer Mutt another treat. Conner praised her for remembering how he'd shown her to do it right. "Thank you for the goodies, ladies. Mutt and I both appreciate it."

He stacked his plate on top of Mutt's and gave the dog's leash a tug. "Take care, you two."

When he and Mutt had circled around the hedge to his driveway, Jody called after him, "Hey, Conner, stay safe out there."

There was a hint of worry in her voice, as if she really was concerned about the kinds of situations that people in law enforcement faced on a daily basis. He wasn't sure what to make of that. Other than his grandfather, he couldn't remember anyone outside of his coworkers who cared about the dangers inherent in Conner's job.

While her concern didn't feel comfortable, it did feel nice. Maybe.

Not knowing how else to respond, he nodded and waved one last time before taking refuge in his house.

It was Sunday morning, and Jody had a tough decision to make. She hated to miss church, but this was the first time she had another person to figure into the equation. At least Conner had called to say the police were still at a loss as to who had attacked Mrs. Caldwell. There had been two other similar incidents in the same area, and neither of those victims had any ties to the social services department. They were operating under the assumption that it had been a crime of opportunity. While that was reassuring, she was sorry to learn other people had been injured.

So her hesitation about going to church was more about how Mia would handle attending services with a bunch of strangers, especially when she still wasn't talking. The little girl had gotten used to Jody saying grace before meals, but it was obvious that it was her first experience with the practice. When asked if she'd ever been to church, Mia had only looked confused by the question and went back to coloring.

There were other risks as well. Detective Galloway had checked in with her yesterday after he'd heard about the attack on Mrs. Caldwell. He'd also wanted to see if Mia had started talking, but he'd let Jody know that there hadn't been any progress in the case. Until they found some answers, there was no way to know if the little girl was safe out in public. In the end, Jody decided to put the matter right where it belonged—in God's hands. She almost always went to the eleven o'clock service, but there were usually far fewer people at eight o'clock. If they went to the smaller gathering, maybe it wouldn't be so overwhelming.

Her decision made, she explained where they were going and what would happen when they got there. After breakfast, she combed Mia's hair and let her decide whether Jody should put it up in pigtails or a ponytail. Mia loved the bright yellow sundress Jody had bought for her, twirling in front of the mirror to see it better.

As they pulled out of the driveway, Jody noticed that Conner's car was gone. It seemed early for him to be out and about. Since he worked evenings, she thought he usually slept later than this. They hadn't seen him or Mutt since their trip to the park. Mia wasn't the only one who felt a little disappointed about that. Jody couldn't remember when she'd last spent time with an attractive man. Most of the men she met through her job were the parents of her students. And while she loved her church, she hadn't met all that many eligible men there. That was a problem for another day.

As she drove into the church parking lot, she went over the situation with Mia one last time. "Okay, we're here. Like I told you before, this is the church I attend every Sunday. We'll be sitting in a big room with other people and listening as the pastor…that's a kind of teacher…talks about the Scriptures. There will be music and times when we pray together."

When she glanced in the rearview mirror, Mia held her hands together like she did when Jody said grace before meals. "That's right, Mia. That's what we'll do."

It was a relief to see that other people were still filing into the building. She'd been worried they'd be late. This way they could be all settled in their seats before the service started. She quickly parked the car and then helped Mia out of her booster seat. "Okay, little one, let's go."

They walked into the building, pausing at the entrance of the sanctuary to look around. Jody started down the center aisle, aiming for the pew where she normally sat near the front. Without warning, Mia dug in her heels and refused to take another step. Worried that she might have made the wrong decision about bringing her to church, Jody leaned down and asked, "Is something wrong, honey?"

Naturally, she didn't answer. Instead, Mia shook her head as she pulled free of Jody's grasp and took off at a run back the way they'd come. After cutting across to the side aisle, Mia stopped beside the second pew from the back. What was going on? They were drawing unwanted attention from the other members of the congregation, but all Jody could do was offer them an apologetic smile as she hustled to catch up with her.

"Mia, I usually sit up front."

It wasn't until Mia pointed that Jody finally noticed a familiar face sitting at the far side of the pew—Conner Dunne. Before Jody could stop her, Mia headed into the near end of the pew. The handful of people who were between her and her intended target good-naturedly stood to let the little girl pass, which left Jody no choice but to follow.

"Sorry, sorry, sorry," she whispered as she squeezed past everyone. By the time she'd reached Mia, the little girl had made herself comfortable next to Conner. At least he seemed more amused than bothered by the kerfuffle. Before she could say anything, the choir stood and began the opening hymn. Mia sat wide-eyed as everyone joined in, including Conner. He knew all the words without having to glance at the hymnal, so maybe he attended this service regularly.

When Mia noticed how Jody was sharing her

hymnal with the lady next to her, Mia tugged on Conner's arm. He gave her a puzzled look, so she tugged his arm again. Finally, he moved the hymnal in her direction, letting her support one side while he held the other. Jody needed to have a talk with the little girl about Conner. Just because they were neighbors and he owned Mia's furry friend, they really shouldn't intrude on his privacy like this.

But as the service continued, Conner continued to accommodate the little girl's demands, even lifting her up to stand on the pew when everyone rose to their feet. He might not have a lot of experience being around kids, but he definitely had a knack for figuring out what Mia wanted.

Jody would have to thank him after the service for making the little girl feel so welcome. After the final hymn was sung, everyone filed out of the pew. Jody usually hung around for coffee and cookies after the service, but she suspected Mia had had enough for one morning.

They followed Conner into the narthex at the front of the church, where the pastor waited to greet people as they filed out. He shook Pastor Dahl's hand. "Nice sermon today, sir."

"Thank you, Deputy Dunne. Glad you could make it this morning."

As Conner moved past, the minister turned his attention to Jody. "I see you brought a friend with you today."

"Mia is my special houseguest."

Pastor Dahl had provided a character reference for Jody when she applied to become a foster parent. He studied the little girl briefly before gently placing his hand on her head to offer a blessing. Mia's eyes flared wide at his touch, but she made no effort to duck away. That didn't surprise Jody; there was something so gentle and reassuring about Pastor Dahl. She'd been drawn to the kindness in his eyes from the first moment they'd met.

"I hope we see you again soon, Mia."

There wasn't much Jody could say to that when she had no idea how long Mia would be staying with her. Not wanting to dwell on how empty her house would feel without the little girl's presence, she smiled at the pastor. "I hope you will, too."

At some point during the conversation, Conner had abandoned them without her noticing. Mia had, though, and was waving like crazy as he drove by. He nodded and waved back as he drove out of the parking lot. Jody couldn't help but be a bit disappointed when he turned in the opposite direction of their neighborhood.

She would've liked to at least thank him for his patience with Mia. Maybe he and Mutt would stop by later, but somehow she doubted it.

"Come on, Mia. We need to pick up a few things at the grocery store on the way home."

When they reached the car, Mia planted herself in front of the open door and held her hand up in the air, her fingers pressed together. Then she pretended to eat something, chomping her teeth and doing a fair imitation of Mutt.

Jody did her best to interpret. "You want to buy more treats for Mutt since Deputy Dunne took the ones we had home with them."

After jerking her head in an emphatic nod, Mia scrambled up on her booster seat. "Okay, but remember that Deputy Dunne has his own errands to run, and he works a lot. I'm not sure when we'll see him and Mutt again."

Or even if.

"Do you understand?"

Mia crossed her arms over her chest and frowned as she shook her head in clear denial. Jody didn't know what else to say. She wasn't any happier about it than Mia. She'd enjoyed the time the four of them had spent together. But her focus needed to be on Mia's well-being. Maybe it would be better to avoid any more interactions with Conner and Mutt. It wasn't fair to Mia to let her get so involved with them.

With her situation so up in the air, there was no telling when the police would find her real family. Depending on the circumstances, the little girl might be removed from Jody's home with little or no notice. The fewer individuals Mia became attached to in the interim, the easier it might be for her when it came time to transition back to her other life.

Jody hoped Mia would remember their time together fondly, but she didn't want their eventual separation to be painful for the little girl. If her attachment to Conner and Mutt continued on its current path, it would only make things worse.

Her mind whirling in circles of indecision, Jody started the car and headed for the pet store despite her misgivings. All she could do was trust in God's infinite wisdom and that He would continue to guide her steps in the coming days.

SIX

Conner went from sound asleep to wide-awake in a heartbeat. Jerking upright, he reached for his phone and swiped across the screen to accept the call. "Dunne here."

"It's Jody. Someone tried to break into my house."

"Where?"

"Out back. The kitchen door."

He put the call on speakerphone so he could yank on last night's uniform and get his service weapon out of the lockbox. "Did you call 9-1-1?"

"Yes, but they said it could be twenty minutes before someone gets here."

"I'm on my way. Lock yourself and Mia in the bathroom. Get down on the floor and stay there until I arrive."

"How will you get inside?"

Good question. He'd rather not have to kick down the door. He'd do it, though, if it came to that. "Can you still hear someone trying to get in?"

For several seconds, the only sound coming over

the call was the rapid gasps of Jody's panicky breathing. "I don't think so."

"Okay, I'm on my way with Mutt. If the suspect is gone, I'll call you back and tell you it's okay to open the door."

"And if they're not?"

"Then I'll handle the situation. Once you're in the bathroom, call 9-1-1 back and tell them that I'm responding."

"I will."

He slipped on his duty vest and picked up his gun before quietly letting himself and Mutt out through the front door. It wasn't exactly legal for him to use Mutt in his former capacity as a police dog, but right now Conner didn't care. He'd do whatever was necessary to protect Mia and Jody. If things went badly, he'd deal with the consequences.

"*Fuss*, Mutt."

The dog followed the command to heel and kept pace with Conner rather than racing ahead. There was no movement outside the front of the house. So far, so good. They circled around to the gate near the back of the garage, where Conner did his best to lift the latch quietly. Swinging the gate open, he stepped through, yelling, "Police! Freeze!"

The moon overhead provided enough light to see that there was no one standing near Jody's back door. Mutt growled low in his chest as Conner pulled out his flashlight and used its bright beam to scan the yard, taking care to check out the deep shadows along the fence. It was time to put Mutt's superpowers to work.

He led the dog over to the door and let him get a good sniff of the area. "*Voran*, boy."

Mutt immediately put his nose to the ground and began the search. After examining the door, he circled the patio, stopping to sniff around a broken flowerpot. The dirt had spilled over the edge of the patio onto the grass, and the flowers were scattered and broken. Conner knew Jody would hate that.

From there, Mutt started across the grass to the back edge of the yard. At the fence, he turned right and followed it to the far corner before reversing course to the opposite side of the yard. Turning back again, he stopped near the center of the fence and sat down. Then he glanced back at Conner and awaited further orders.

It was tempting to turn Mutt loose, but that wouldn't be smart. Besides, Jody and Mia shouldn't be left huddling in the bathroom for any longer than absolutely necessary. Chances were the suspect had left a vehicle parked somewhere on the far side of the trees and was long gone by now. "*Fuss*, Mutt."

The dog gave the top of the fence one last look before reluctantly giving up the hunt. He fell into step with Conner as he made one last sweep around the backyard and then did the same in the front before calling Jody. "All clear. Let me in."

He positioned himself in front of the narrow window by her front door so she could see him. When the door opened, she was as pale as a ghost and shaking. He didn't know how much Mia understood about what had Jody so upset, but her own face was blotchy and streaked with tears. It said a lot about how upset she was that she hadn't yet noticed that Mutt was there.

Conner locked the door and gently guided the pair over to the kitchen table, where Jody settled in a chair with Mia in her lap. They watched in wide-eyed silence as he filled the kettle with water. He put it on the stove to heat and then rummaged around in the cabinets until he found the herbal tea she'd served the night he'd responded to Mia's screams.

"I'll call in an update on the situation."

He'd no sooner said the words than flashing lights lit up the front of the house. "Never mind. I'll be right back."

He flipped on the porch light to make sure the responding officer could see him and then waited in front of the garage for her to join him. "I live next door. Ms. Kruse called me after she called 9-1-1."

He often shared patrol with Sheila Stark and had gotten to know her pretty well in the short time he'd been on the job. She had a knack for dealing with people of all kinds, but that didn't mean she couldn't play hardball if the occasion called for it.

"What's the situation?"

"Not sure. She reported hearing someone in the backyard. Evidently it sounded like they were trying to break in through the kitchen door, which opens out onto her patio. The only thing I saw out back was a broken flowerpot on the patio."

He looked around for Mutt, but he must have stayed inside with Jody and Mia. The dog obviously had his own priorities. "You might not know that my German shepherd is a retired K-9 dog. Mutt followed a scent from the patio to a spot near the center of the back fence. You might see his paw prints in the dirt, but I didn't step into the flower bed back there."

Sheila was busy taking notes. "So the homeowner heard a noise but didn't actually see anybody?"

"I think so, but I haven't had a chance to talk to her in any detail. She and the little girl she fosters are both pretty shaken up. I was about to make her a cup of tea when you arrived."

Sheila gave him an odd look. Probably because making drinks for the victims wasn't something officers responding to a scene normally did. Hopefully, she'd write it off to the fact that he and Jody were neighbors. "Anything I should know about the kid? What's her situation?"

"I'm guessing you heard about the little girl found abandoned at the hospital? That was Mia, or at least that's what they're calling her. She hasn't said a word since they found her. If you need to know more, Detective Galloway is handling the investigation. We don't know if this incident is related to the case, but he'll want to know about it anyway."

"I'll give him a call tomorrow and send him a copy of the report. It won't hurt to cover all bases."

She put her notebook away. "Meanwhile, I'll take a look around and then join you inside."

"Sounds good."

The kettle was boiling away when he walked in, but Jody wasn't reacting to its shrill whistle at all. She sat staring at the back door, but he wasn't convinced she was registering anything else around her. He poured the water over the tea bag in a large mug and added two teaspoons of sugar to the mix. While the tea steeped, he checked the fridge for one of those juice boxes that Mia liked. He picked a flavor at random, shoved the straw in the top and then set it on the table.

"Mia, why don't you move over to this chair and drink this?"

He waited until she was settled in the other seat before setting the hot tea in front of Jody. "Sip this. It's hot."

It took her longer to respond than he liked, but she finally reached for the tea. "Thank you."

He took the chair opposite Mia and next to where Jody sat at the end of the table. Both Jody and Mia looked pale and badly shaken. He dealt with people like this all too often and hated knowing that it would be some time before either of them felt completely safe again. He was furious that someone had scared them both so badly, especially after what Mia had already been through. When Jody shivered, he was instantly up and looking around for something to keep her warm. He spotted a patchwork blanket tossed over the arm of the couch and wrapped it around her shoulders. From there, he went down the hall to Mia's bedroom and got a smaller quilt for her.

When he returned, Mia had finally realized her furry friend was there. Mutt had laid his head in her lap. She sipped her juice and stroked his fur while Jody watched them with haunted eyes. "Who would do such a thing?"

He gave her the honest answer. "Right now we don't know. Deputy Stark is taking another look around before she comes in."

A few seconds later, there was a sharp rap on the front door. He stood before Jody had a chance to move. "I'll let her in."

When Sheila stepped inside, he performed the introductions. "Deputy Sheila Stark, this is Jody Kruse, Mia and that's Mutt."

She gave the dog a long look and stayed right where she was. "He's huge. How friendly is he?"

Considering the dog's size, it wasn't a surprise that she might be cautious about approaching him. "Mutt, come here."

The dog reluctantly abandoned his little friend long enough to join Conner and Sheila by the door. He sat down and waited for Conner to perform introductions. "Mutt, this is Deputy Stark. Sheila, this is Mutt, retired K-9 dog."

When Mutt stood up, she cautiously let him sniff her hand and then gently patted him on the head. With the social amenities over, Mutt retreated to sit at Mia's side. Sheila watched him for a few seconds more. "I didn't know you used to work K-9."

"I didn't, but I was friends with his handler and got to know Mutt through him. When Mutt retired, Justin couldn't keep him. Since the dog knew me, I offered to take him."

"Lucky Mutt."

"Lucky me. He's a great dog."

"Your little neighbor sure thinks so."

It was time to get back to business. He led Sheila over to the table. She took the chair at the opposite end from Jody. Rather than sitting down, Conner leaned against the kitchen counter where he could keep an eye on Mia and Mutt while Sheila completed her report. It didn't take long. Without anything more to go on other than a flowerpot getting knocked over, there wasn't much the police could do.

Sheila gave Jody one of her cards. "Call if you need anything."

Turning to Conner, she said, "Since you live next door, would you mind taking a look around the back-yard and maybe on the other side of the fence in the daylight? I'd like to know if there are any footprints or if there's a chance it was a critter of some kind."

Jody looked as if she was about to protest that last suggestion, but Conner hastened to reassure her. "She's not questioning your story, Jody. But we need to consider every possibility."

He wasn't sure he'd actually helped matters, but she finally stood and held her hand out to Sheila.

"Thank you for coming so quickly, Deputy Stark. I really appreciate it."

"Anytime."

Conner escorted Sheila back outside. Before getting into her cruiser, she asked one more question. "How well do you know her?"

He shrugged. "I only moved into the neighborhood a couple of weeks ago. We hadn't even spoken until Mia woke Mutt up in the middle of the night screaming in terror. She had nightmares when she first moved in with Jody. I called it in as a possible domestic dispute and responded since I was close. She's been doing better lately."

He stared back at the house, wondering if tonight's events would trigger a new round of screaming. He hoped not, for everyone's sake. "Since they have no idea who abandoned Mia at the hospital or why, I try to keep an eye on things. There's also the fact her caseworker was assaulted not long after she'd stopped by to talk to me and Jody. There's no proof it's related to this case, but it could be."

Sheila's expression turned grim. "Poor kid. Like I said, I'll shoot Galloway a copy of the report. Call me if you see anything suspicious along the fence."

"Will do. See you soon."

He waited until she'd driven out of sight before going back inside, unsure what to do next. It was a sure bet Jody would have a hard time going back to sleep after everything that had happened. Mia would likely have problems, too, but maybe not if she had

Mutt to watch over her. Should he leave the dog and go back home?

In the time he'd been outside, Jody and Mia had moved to a big upholstered chair in the living room. They were both wrapped in the quilts with Mutt stretched out on the floor at Jody's feet.

He took a seat on the couch. "Are you okay?"

"Not really." There was a brief flash of anger in her eyes. "She thinks some critter broke the flowerpot, doesn't she?"

"Not necessarily. Otherwise she wouldn't have asked me to check the area in the daylight. It's impossible to see anything out there right now even with a flashlight. I promise Mutt and I will take a good look around first thing in the morning."

"I appreciate it." She adjusted the blanket to cover Mia a little better. "We'll be fine. You should go home and get some sleep."

As soon as she said that, Mia whimpered as her chin wobbled and her eyes filled up with tears. It would take a far colder heart than Conner's to walk away and leave them alone to deal with their fear alone. He hadn't seen either of them for more than a week. Finding out that he and Jody attended the same church had come as a bit of a shock. He'd been going there since he'd first moved to town, but he'd never seen her there before. He would've remembered if he had.

He'd walked away while Jody and the pastor talked, planning to head for a nearby diner that served the best breakfasts around. He and other members of local law enforcement often hung out there after a late shift or before reporting in for an early one. If he'd lingered outside the church any longer, he would've given in to the urge to ask Jody if she and Mia would like to come with him. That could have certainly set off a round of gossip at work he really didn't want to have to deal with.

He'd also been called back to Seattle one last time for an ongoing trial. Crossing back over Stevens Pass from Seattle to eastern Washington, he'd had plenty of time to think about his growing involvement with Jody and her little ward. After much mental hemming and hawing, he'd decided that they would all be best served if he maintained a professional distance.

He'd had to wonder if Mia would be still living with Jody when he returned. If they'd found her family, she would likely already be gone. He would've regretted not having a chance to say goodbye and tell her that he smiled every time he saw the portrait of him and Mutt hanging on his refrigerator.

And he had no idea how he would be able to explain to Mutt why his little friend had disappeared. The dog had already gone through the trauma of losing his longtime partner. He didn't need to lose another of his favorite humans so soon. Considering how attached Mia was to Mutt, it would only hurt more if she continued to spend more time with him.

However, his conscience reminded him that she'd already had a rough night. He'd never forgive himself if taking Mutt home triggered another round of Mia's nighttime terrors. Stifling the urge to sigh, he made an offer he was sure he would regret. "Look, since I'm already here, I'll crash on your couch for what's left of the night. Things will seem better in the morning."

That was probably an overly optimistic assessment of the situation. That Jody didn't even hesitate to accept his offer made it all too clear how frightened she was. "I'll get you a pillow and a blanket. I'll tuck Mia in her bed and be right back."

As Jody led her away, Mia kept looking back at him. She might not have said a word, but the fear in her eyes said all too much. Mutt stared at Conner for a few seconds and then quietly padded down the hall to Mia's room.

Five hours later, Conner woke up staring at a strange ceiling. Feeling a bit thickheaded, it took him a second to remember where he was and why— on Jody's couch, because someone had tried to break into her house. His back hurt from sleeping in one position too long, but a few stretches would take care of that. His main problem was that, once again, he'd gone way beyond what his duty required of him, and he didn't know how to get back on the right side of that line. Maybe it was cowardly of him, but Conner liked his solitary life. Getting out of the place before he had to face Jody or interact with Mia would be a good place to start rebuilding the wall between them.

He'd tried not to think about how right it had felt that day at church with Mia sitting next to him, insisting on holding the hymnal she was too young to read. When the congregation rose to its feet, he'd automatically lifted her up on the pew next to him so she could see better. Another reason he'd taken off right after the service was that he'd been flashing back to vague memories of going to church with his own parents. He'd always sat between them. Sometimes he'd shared the hymnal with his mom, sometimes with his dad, but always as a family.

To this day, he missed them with an ache that had eased but never healed. He loved his grandfather, too, and thanked God regularly for the gift Jasper had been in Conner's life. Not only had the two of them bonded as grandson and grandfather, they also shared a loss that had been unique to them. The loss of his son and daughter-in-law had dealt Jasper a heavy blow, but he'd pushed beyond his own pain to help Conner deal with his.

He suspected Jasper had never remarried after his wife died because he'd never wanted to risk hurting that much again. Up until now, Conner had thought the old man had the right of it, but he was starting to have doubts.

Yeah, the smart thing to do was to put on his shoes, retrieve his dog and then slip out before Jody and Mia woke up. Before going back to his house, he'd take care of the reconnaissance that Sheila had asked him to do and send her a message with his findings. What happened after that would all depend on what he found.

Either way, his conscience would be clear because he'd done his job. That's what was important. Jody would understand that he had his own life with things to do, places to be. Besides, comforting Mia was her responsibility. If she needed help, that's what the social workers were for. If it turned out that someone really had tried to break in, it would be up to Detective Galloway to decide what measures to take.

His decision made, he swung his legs over, intending to sit up when he realized that he was about to step on Mia. One look at the situation and all his plans went right down the drain. The little girl was sound asleep on the floor between the couch and the coffee table. Mutt had wedged himself under the table in order to stay next to her. And if that wasn't a big enough signal that Mia took comfort not only from having the dog close by but from Conner's presence as well, she was using his uniform shirt as a blanket.

So much for protecting himself emotionally, which was driving his need to reestablish some distance. Walking away now would bruise that sweet little girl's heart, and there was no way Conner could do that and live with himself. Grandpa Jasper had stepped up when Conner had needed him the most. If he wanted to be the kind of man his grandfather would respect, he needed to follow the old man's example. Instead of worrying about protecting himself, he'd let God guide his footsteps.

And maybe he'd start by taking Mia and Jody to the diner for breakfast.

SEVEN

Jody and Mia watched from the patio while Conner and Mutt explored the back edge of the yard. They were trying to determine if it had been a two-legged intruder or a four-legged critter that had tried to break into her house. He'd stopped to take several pictures of one particular spot along the way. Finally, he'd carefully stepped across the flower bed to study the fence up close while Mutt kept snuffling around in the dirt at his feet. That alone would've told her that was where the trail from the patio had led.

It appeared that the intruder had come into her yard over the fence. Did that make it more likely that a raccoon had decided to pay her patio a visit? It wouldn't be the first time she'd spotted one of the masked bandits waddling across her yard after dark. On one level, she almost hoped Conner had found paw prints back there. She'd be embarrassed for dragging two different deputies to her house in the middle of the night, but at least she'd be able to sleep better. Mia, too, for that matter.

Conner put his hands on the top of the fence and pulled himself up and over to drop down on the other side. At the same time, Mutt backed away far enough to gain some running room. In an amazing display of strength and grace, he flew up and over the six-foot fence to join his master on the other side. Mia's eyes lit up as she clapped her hands in excitement.

"You're right, Mia, that was amazing."

Just like their breakfast outing had been. Jody thought it was funny that she'd lived in town far longer than Conner, yet she'd never even heard of the diner he'd taken them to earlier. Apparently, it was a frequent hangout for members of local law enforcement. The food had been fabulous and his coworkers friendly.

Meanwhile, he and Mutt had made it all the way out to the trees and disappeared from sight only to return a short time later. By that point, they looked more relaxed, their attention no longer focused on the ground. Mia clapped her hands as Mutt flew over the fence again, clearing it with ease. It took Conner a little more effort, but Mia generously applauded for him, too. Jody laughed and joined in the celebration.

Both dog and man looked pleased by their audience's enthusiastic approval. Conner looked down at Mia and then pointed toward a stainless steel bowl he'd left on the patio. "Do Mutt a favor and add some water to his bowl. Hopping fences is thirsty work."

She was off like a shot. Earlier, Conner had shown her how to turn on the hose at a trickle and let her fill the bowl. This time, she got almost as much water on her shoes and pants as she did in the bowl, but she got the job done. She kept Mutt company while he consumed an incredible amount of the water. When he stepped back, she topped off the bowl a second time before turning the hose off.

While all that was going on, Jody was aware of Conner sidling closer. She gave him a quick glance and then asked, "What did you find?"

He frowned. "Nothing definitive. There's a lot of undergrowth under the trees, so I couldn't pick out any clear footprints. Mutt was able to follow the scent trail a short distance into the woods, but then it got muddled, judging by the way he was acting. The ground is pretty wet thanks to the rain during the night."

That was disappointing. "How about here in the yard?"

He led her over to the back fence and pointed toward the ground. "The mulch has been disturbed here, so someone walked through the flower bed. But again, it could have been a squirrel burying nuts."

She noticed another of her plants had a broken stem and pointed it out to Conner. "This isn't the first time one of my plants has been damaged like that. The last time it was two of the new perennials I planted back in the spring. They were pretty much flattened. Since I have the area around the plants and bushes covered with bark mulch to keep the weeds down, I couldn't see any footprints. At the time, I thought that maybe Mia had accidently stepped on them. I noticed it the day that Mutt came sailing over the fence to hang out with Mia."

He snapped a picture of the damaged plant. "Where were the other two?"

She pointed to a blank space in the bark. "They were about there. They didn't recover from the damage, so I pulled them out."

"So same general area as that one and near the same section of fence."

It wasn't exactly a question, but she nodded anyway. "What do you think it all means?"

From the tension in his stance, she wasn't going to be very happy about his answer. "There's nothing much to go on. A broken planter on the patio, a couple of plants that may have been stepped on, a scent trail that leads from your fence to the woods. They could all be explained by an animal nosing around looking for something to eat rather than some person prowling around."

She shivered despite the bright sunshine. "So the bottom line is there's nothing police can do."

He didn't look any happier about that than she did. "I know it's not what you want to hear, but I'd rather be honest with you. Added all together, it does sound suspicious, but we don't have the manpower to station someone outside your house 24-7. However, Sheila promised to notify Detective Galloway about what happened last night. Knowing her, she'll also probably stop by again to check on you and Mia.

I'll call her later to update her on what Mutt and I saw today."

"Thanks."

She realized that she hadn't actually sounded all that grateful. "I'm sorry, Conner. I know that you've gone above and beyond for Mia. I really do appreciate it."

He stepped closer as his expression softened. "It wasn't only because of Mia. I don't like seeing anyone scared, but especially women and children."

Which is what made him so good at his job. "I'm fine. Really."

She glanced over to check on Mia and Mutt. They sat side by side on the patio, the dog looking content as Mia stroked his fur. "Those two have become best buddies."

Conner was watching them, too. After a second, he drew in a deep breath and slowly let it out. "Listen, don't take this wrong, but I keep wondering if it's a good idea to let them spend so much time together."

His concern echoed her own on the subject. "You're worried about her getting too attached to him. I've had the same thoughts."

"Yeah, but I figure it's probably already too late. She'll miss Mutt one way or the other. The poor guy is going to miss her, too. He already lost his original owner, and that was hard on him. I can't remember if I told you that the police officer he worked with on the job couldn't keep Mutt. Justin had to move out of state to help care for his parents. Since the dog already knew me, I offered to take him even though I'm definitely second string."

"Don't sell yourself short. Mutt was lucky you stepped up to give him a good home. He's clearly happy living with you."

Conner looked a little embarrassed by her comments. "Thanks for saying that."

After a bit, he started talking again. "But back to Mia. We have no idea what her life was like before she came to live with you. On the whole, she acts like a happy kid. Even though she was scared last night, she seems to be adjusting well to living with you." He looked back toward Mia. "You haven't mentioned her screaming lately. I'm guessing that's stopped, since Mutt isn't pitching fits every night."

"She still wakes up some nights, though. Since she still isn't talking, I put a bell by her bed that she rings if she needs me. I sit with her for a few minutes and maybe read a book or two. That usually does the trick, and she goes back to sleep more quickly."

"That's good, but it's too bad she's still not talking."

"The counselor said that could take time, but I can't help but worry. I just wish there was something more I could be doing to help her."

The corner of Conner's mouth quirked up in a small grin. "Now who's selling herself short? The counselor and the caseworker haven't gotten her to talk, and both of them have years of experience and training working with kids like Mia. She clearly trusts you, and you've given her a safe harbor until the authorities find her family."

"And if they never do? What happens then? Believe me when I say that being abandoned has long-lasting consequences."

The words slipped out before she could stop them. She regretted it even more when Conner spoke. "It sounds like you have some personal experience with that."

The gentle concern in his voice was almost her undoing. Rather than deny it, she reluctantly went with the truth. "I do, but it was more like my parents left me out on the curb with a Free to a Good Home sign. Sometimes the headlines make it sound as if only poor kids are abused or neglected. My folks had plenty of money, and they lived to spend it. Just not on me. Evidently having me was an unhappy accident, one that really cramped their style. They'd leave money on the table and take off for a weekend, sometimes longer."

"How old were you?"

"The first time I was probably around eight or nine."

Conner went from looking curious to sporting his full-on cop face as soon as the words were out of her mouth. "Tell me someone put a stop to that immediately."

For some reason, she found the amount of anger in his response surprising. She'd hate to be on the receiving end of it, but she knew he wasn't going to like her answer. "How was I to know that other parents didn't do stuff like that? After a while, even after I knew it wasn't right, I was too embarrassed to say anything."

"What happened to change things?"

"I needed a permission slip signed for a field trip at school. I was supposed to get one of my parents to sign it, but they'd unexpectedly left on another junket while I was at school. My homeroom teacher suspected I'd forged my mom's signature and sent me to the office. When I confessed they were out of town, the principal asked who was taking care of me. That's when CPS stepped in."

He lifted his hand as if to offer the comfort of his touch but at the last second let it drop back down to his side and took a step back. "I'm sorry you went through all of that."

As always, thinking about her foster parents brought a smile to her face. "Don't be. I was one of the lucky ones and got a great placement right out of the gate. Seriously, I loved my foster parents almost from the very start. The Burks showed me what a family was meant to be. They treated me like one of their own kids and included me in all of their family activities, including going to church. Finding them and finding God changed my life in so many ways. With their help, I learned how to trust people, how to love."

"And that's why you became a teacher, not to mention a foster parent."

"Yep. I love helping kids find success." She paused to look in Mia's direction. "And I feel God has led me to open my home to a child who needed a safe haven. Of course, some foster kids only need a place to stay short-term. You know, like if their parent is in the hospital. But with someone like Mia, there's no telling how long she'll need to be here. As far as I'm concerned, she can remain in my home for however long she needs me."

"She's a lucky little girl to have you."

"Yes, but she also has Mutt and you. Not every little girl has her very own deputy and highly trained police dog living right next door."

He laughed. "And on that note, I need to get ready for work. I'll update Sheila and see if Detective Galloway had anything interesting to say. I'll also see what he's learned about Mrs. Caldwell's condition and what happened to her."

She'd been about to ask him to do that. It was like he could read her mind. "Thanks for everything you've done."

He'd been heading in Mutt's direction, but he stopped to look back at her. "It's my job."

She remained where she was, trying to deal with the short burst of hurt that his blunt statement had caused. Yes, it was his job to protect. She knew that. But what she hadn't known until that moment was that a small part of her heart really wished his reasons for his determined efforts to protect both her and Mia were a little bit personal, too.

After a slight hesitation, she called after him, "Deputy Dunne, stay safe out there."

When Conner got to work, there was a message for him to stop by Galloway's office before hitting the road. Maybe there'd been a break in the case, but he wasn't holding out much hope that they'd been that lucky.

Once again, he knocked on the door frame and waited for the detective to wave him in. "Come on in, Conner, and have a seat. This won't take long."

Galloway started talking the second Conner was settled into his chair. "I talked to Deputy Stark earlier today about what happened last night. She said you were going to take another look around in the daylight."

"I did. I wish I had some definitive answers for you."

He didn't bother to disguise his frustration, and Galloway wouldn't appreciate him being anything less than honest. "There was a broken flowerpot on the patio. Mutt followed a scent trail that led straight from there to the back fence. A plant was damaged in the same area. Unfortunately, the ground is covered with bark mulch, so no footprints. After Mutt and I hopped the fence, he followed the trail out to the greenbelt behind our houses but lost it after that."

Galloway leaned back in his chair and met Conner's gaze head-on. "Deputy Stark said based on the evidence, she would've been inclined to think an animal of some kind knocked over a flowerpot. But considering the little girl's situation, she wasn't so sure. Does that line up with your thinking?"

"Yeah, pretty much."

Conner paused to consider how much more to tell him. Despite his earlier comment to Jody that he was doing his job, he couldn't keep fooling himself. Maybe proximity had something to do with it, but he was far more involved in the situation than he would've been under other circumstances. "There's a couple of other things that Detective Stark isn't aware of. When I was looking around the backyard, Ms. Kruse told me that a while back she'd noticed two other plants in the same general area of the yard had been crushed. At the time, she thought maybe Mia had wandered into the flower bed and accidently stepped on them. Now she's not so sure. At this point in time, there's no way to know how it happened."

Galloway stopped taking notes and looked up at him questioningly. "There's more than that."

"Yeah, maybe. The little girl has gotten rather attached to my dog. Ms. Kruse and Mia wanted to check out the playground at a nearby park, so Mutt and I went with them."

Doing his best to ignore the curious look Galloway shot in his direction, he kept talking. "I got one of those strange feelings. You know, like someone is staring at you. At about the same moment, Mutt quit watching Mia playing on the climber and went on point, staring off across the park. I didn't see anyone who stuck out, but he and I did a quick patrol of the area just in case. We didn't find anything, but I got the same feeling as we walked back home."

"So it's the same kind of deal. Under other circumstances, you wouldn't think much of it."

"Yeah."

"Too bad the dog doesn't talk."

Conner huffed a small laugh. "It's not the first time I've had the same thought."

"Anything else?"

"Yeah, we were walking home when Jody told me about what happened to the caseworker not long after she stopped by to talk with me. That might account for why I got a bit spooked after we left the park."

"That's understandable. Last I heard, she still wasn't conscious, but the doctors are hopeful. Until that happens, there's not much chance of anyone being able to link the attack to her job, much less a specific case."

Galloway dropped his pen on the desk. "On a happier note, we've gotten a few reports back from the lab. They picked up the little girl's DNA as well as one unidentified male on the backpack. From the markers they have in common, it's most likely her father. That's the good news. The bad news is that he's not in the system. They're looking for other possible family members, but so far no luck."

That was disappointing. If they'd been able to identify her father, they'd be a whole lot closer to knowing both Mia's real name and the family situation.

The detective was still talking. "It was a long shot, anyway. Still, his info is in the system now. If he pops up again, we'll have him. On another subject, from what I've heard, Mia still isn't talking."

"Not so far. Jody says Mia is sleeping better at night. No more screaming, anyway. She was pretty upset by everything last night. They both were."

"Can't blame them for that."

Conner checked the time. "I should be going. Let me know if there's anything I can do to help with your investigation."

"You're already doing more than I expected."

Conner wasn't sure if the detective was grateful about that. "I'm doing my job."

It was the same answer he'd given Jody, and he'd been lying both times. When it came to protecting Jody and Mia, it wasn't simply his job. It was personal.

EIGHT

Two days later, Jody stood at the back door and stared out into the darkness. The only source of light inside the house came from the night-lights in the hallway and in Mia's room. If anyone was watching the house, it would appear that they'd both gone to bed. Actually, that was true for Mia. Jody had tucked her in at eight o'clock after reading several chapters from a children's book of Bible stories.

Mia seemed to enjoy them. But when Jody closed the book and set it on the small bookcase near the bed, the little minx pulled another book out from under her pillow and held it out with a hopeful look on her face. It was all Jody could do not to groan. They'd stopped at a bookstore yesterday so Mia could pick out a new book. As soon as she'd spotted the one with a German shepherd on the cover, she'd refused to consider any other options. That would've been fine if she hadn't been insisting Jody read it to her at every possible opportunity.

After plowing through it yet again, she'd turned out the light on the bedside table to signal that reading time was over. Then they'd said prayers. Well, she'd said hers while Mia listened. When Jody finished, she'd encouraged Mia to silently say one for those who were important to her. Mia had closed her eyes, her lips moving in silence for several seconds. Then she held out her arms for a hug. The simple gesture had brought a hint of tears to Jody's eyes. Love given so freely was a gift in anyone's life. She'd given Mia one last kiss on her forehead and left the room.

After paying a few bills and doing some other chores, she'd tried to go to bed herself. Despite her best efforts to relax, sleep remained elusive. Had her house always been so noisy without her noticing? Every small creak, each whisper of a breeze outside her window had her jerking upright as if that would help her distinguish between the normal sounds of the night and the possibility that someone was trying to break in again.

Because no matter what the police thought, she remained convinced that flowerpot hadn't been broken by some random animal. Conner had been right about Deputy Stark stopping by again. She'd stayed just long enough to take a quick look around the backyard, appearing more frustrated than anything. After making sure Jody still had her contact information, she told her not to hesitate to call if anything else happened. Then the deputy was gone, leaving Jody with more questions than answers.

The detective on the case had also called. After telling her that there'd been very little progress on the investigation, Detective Galloway assured her that he'd been made aware of the other night's events. He was sorry it had happened, and he understood that it had probably been pretty scary. Seriously? Only probably scary? It was hard not to be a little bit angry about his attitude, even if the evidence had been pretty sketchy. But Jody understood that the police had a lot on their plate and needed to focus on the cases where they had solid leads.

Conner had been right about the fact that there wouldn't be a police car parked in front of her house to stand guard any time soon. Realistically, she'd never really expected that to happen, which was the reason she was drinking a cup of chamomile tea while standing watch herself.

The call she'd gotten late in the afternoon from Dale Greve also kept playing out in her head. He'd heard about the attempted break-in and wanted to know how both Jody and Mia were holding up. As tempting as it was to claim everything was fine and dandy, that neither of them had been adversely affected by the event, she knew better. After giving her version of the events, she added that thankfully it hadn't triggered another round of Mia screaming during the night.

Mr. Greve was relieved to hear that. He again asked how Jody herself was doing and if she wanted them to consider moving Mia to another foster home if things were getting to be a bit too much. After she assured him of her intention to care for Mia as long as she needed her, he'd thanked Jody for her dedication. He also gave her the date and time for Mia's next appointment with Dr. Mayberry.

It was long past time to be back in bed. Jody took one last look around the backyard, this time turning on the outside lights. She blinked to adjust to the sudden brightness and then scanned the entire yard from right to left and back again. Seeing nothing out of the ordinary, she flipped the lights back off and started toward the hallway that led to Mia's bedroom. The little girl was curled up on her side, sound asleep. At least one of them would wake up well rested in the morning.

She was headed to her bedroom when there was a knock at the front door. Who could that be?

"Jody, it's Conner."

Breathing a sigh of relief, she hustled across to unlock the door. He was still in uniform, making it likely that he'd just gotten back from work. Mutt was at his side, his tail wagging. He looked far happier than his owner, who was breathing hard, as if he'd been running. "I was walking Mutt around the greenbelt out back and saw your patio light flash on and off."

And he'd come running, no doubt because he felt obligated to check on anything suspicious. "I'm sorry if I worried you, Conner. I couldn't sleep, so I fixed myself some chamomile tea. I was about to head back to bed, but I couldn't resist the urge to peek outside before turning in."

His stance relaxed, but he still looked worried. "Did you hear something that woke you up?"

"No, only the usual night sounds." She forced a small smile. "I never realized how much this house creaks and groans."

Redirecting the conversation to a different subject, she asked, "Do you and Mutt often go walking in the woods at night?"

"Actually, we vary the route just to keep things interesting." He patted Mutt on the head. "I don't like leaving him outside while I'm gone, and he needs to burn off some pent-up energy. It also helps me work out some of the kinks that come from sitting in a car for hours at a stretch."

"That makes sense."

A huge yawn hit her with no warning, leaving her embarrassed. Conner grinned. "Seems like the chamomile has done its job. Mutt and I should head home and let you get some sleep."

He was right. "Thanks again for checking in. Good night, Conner. Good night, Mutt."

She was about to close the door when he shuffled his feet but made no move to leave. "Was there something else?"

"If I don't see you before then, maybe I'll see you at church on Sunday. I don't always make it if my shift runs late. So if I'm not there, that's why. Anyway, I thought maybe we could hit the diner again on the way home. You know, if you'd like that."

His offer came as a big surprise, but she didn't hesitate to accept. "I'd like that a lot. I'll let it be a surprise for Mia. No use in getting her hopes up in case you can't make it."

"Okay, see you then."

Then he was gone, disappearing into the darkness with his furry friend. When she sought out her bed, she realized she was still smiling even as sleep overtook her.

The morning sunshine gradually coaxed Conner out of a deep slumber. When he had no luck falling back to sleep, he rolled over onto his back and stared up at the ceiling, his mood a mix of emotions. He hadn't lied to Jody about Mutt needing to blow off some steam after being shut up in the house all day. It was also true that they varied their routes from night to night, but they rarely wandered through the trees behind the houses.

For one thing, short of jumping the fence, they had to go a fair distance to gain access to the greenbelt. He also wasn't fond of stumbling around in the darkness while trying not to trip over tree roots and rocks. After a couple of bruised shins and one nasty cut on his knee, he'd pretty much written off the greenbelt for their walks at night. They'd only been there this time to see if Mutt picked up anything suspicious.

The dog had an incredible memory for scents and would know if the intruder had been back.

They'd been about to turn back the way they'd come when Jody's light flashed on and off. Fearing for the worst, they'd bolted out of the trees across the grass at a dead run. The two of them jumped the fence into their own yard before circling around the front of her house. It hadn't been until he got there that he realized he'd left his weapon at home when he and Mutt left for their walk. What if there had been an intruder? That was a mistake he wouldn't make again.

Most nights all he wanted to do was put the job behind him, drawing a sharp line between work and his home. Taking a walk with Mutt did more than help him stretch a few muscles. Breathing the fresh air and spending time with the undemanding dog helped remind him that there was more to life than handing out speeding tickets, dealing with the aftermath of accidents and responding to 9-1-1 calls.

But right now, with Mia and Jody living with so many uncertainties, it was getting harder and harder to leave the job behind. He'd deliberately lived a pretty solitary life since he'd lost his grandfather, but somehow Jody and that big-eyed little girl had slipped passed all his defenses. He wanted to keep them safe. If that meant pulling a self-assigned second shift to watch over them, so be it.

It wasn't realistic to think he could spend the entire night circling the neighborhood watching for an undefined threat, but he would sleep better if he and Mutt did a quick patrol before turning in. At least Mutt had the scent now. If he picked it up again, it meant the intruder had returned, and Conner would let Detective Galloway know what was going on. It was the best Conner could do until they got a break in the case.

One problem dealt with, Conner's whirling thoughts turned to another subject. What had possessed him to invite Jody and Mia out for brunch after church? The words had popped out of his mouth with no warning. While he didn't exactly regret the offer, it definitely complicated things. For him, anyway.

Looking back, it had been that first day at church with Mia and Jody that started the change in his thinking. Finding little Mia curled up in his uniform shirt for comfort the other night had only reinforced it. The only question was whether he wanted to follow this new path to its end. Or was it already too late to turn back now?

He was saved from having to answer that question when his phone lit up. Before answering he checked the screen and frowned. Why would Galloway be calling him at home? Conner was scheduled to work later in the day, so the detective could've simply left a message to check in with him before Conner left on patrol.

"Dunne here, Detective."

"Sorry if I woke you, Conner, but we might've

had a break in the case. It's too soon to know what it means if anything, so don't tell Ms. Kruse or the case-worker yet. No use in getting everyone all worked up for no reason. I checked in with your supervisor, and he okayed me borrowing you for a couple of hours. If I give you the location, can you meet me there?"

His stomach curled up in a tight knot of tension, Conner rolled up to his feet. "Give me the details. I'll be out the door inside twenty minutes. To save time, I'll come directly from home without going to headquarters first."

"See you when you get here."

After letting Mutt out to take care of business, Conner grabbed a couple of energy bars to eat on the way to the meet-up point and left the coffee brewing while he took a quick shower. Once he was dressed, he fed Mutt and gave him fresh water. The dog had picked up on Conner's tension and prowled from one side of the living room to the other. Even after being retired for more than a year, the dog clearly missed being on the job.

He tossed Mutt a treat. "Sorry, buddy. I know I promised you a long run this morning, but we'll go when I get home."

After filling a to-go cup with coffee, he headed out the door. Just his luck, Jody was standing by her car. She waved, but Mia looked past him toward his house.

"Sorry, Mia, but Mutt has to stay inside. I've been called in to work."

She frowned her disappointment and settled into her booster seat. Jody paused before buckling her in. "Did something happen?"

Hedging his bets, he offered her an answer that was true but didn't offer up any details. "They need extra help with a situation and asked if I could come in early."

Jody finished buckling Mia in and turned to face him. Her concern for him was right there in her dark eyes as she once again said, "Be careful out there, Conner."

"I'll do my best."

He checked his rearview mirror one last time before a bend in the road would take him out of sight of their houses. She was still watching him. As if sensing him looking back, Jody waved one last time and then got into her own car.

It was a thirty-minute drive to the location where Conner was supposed to meet Detective Galloway. The narrow road wound its way through high hills with occasional steep drop-offs plunging down to the valley below while thickets of trees on both sides of the road limited visibility in all directions. As he was rounding a sharp turn, he hit the brakes. Emergency flares were burning on the road in the distance, and a line of orange traffic cones blocked off the lane he was in. Even without those clues, the crime scene tape being strung from tree to tree made it clear he was in the right spot.

After parking on the edge of the road, he grabbed his hat off the passenger seat and got out to study the scene before heading toward the state trooper directing traffic at the near end of the road closure. He waited until the man waved through several cars in the oncoming lane before speaking.

"I'm Deputy Conner Dunne. Detective Jack Galloway is expecting me."

The trooper pointed off to his left, Conner's right. "He's down in that ravine. You can follow the trail of broken trees and bushes. The hillside is steep but doable as long as you're careful going down. The body and the car are both at the bottom. They've been there awhile."

Considering the grim tone in Galloway's voice when he called, Conner had already been suspecting the worst. That didn't mean he was happy about being proven right. After saying a silent prayer for the dead, he took a deep breath and headed into the trees, following the sound of muted voices coming from farther down the slope.

NINE

Galloway stood off to one side with another state trooper watching other people work the scene. Conner stopped to check in with the officer whose job it was to make sure everyone who entered the area signed in and out. It was being treated as a crime scene, not simply as a car accident that had ended tragically.

The vehicle had plunged down the hillside, flipping all the way over on the way. The roof was crushed, the doors on the passenger side bent and twisted, but the driver's door hung open. Apparently the victim had survived long enough to crawl out of the wreck. The poor guy hadn't gotten very far, but at least he'd made it out. It could've been worse, since the car had partially burned after it finished rolling.

Considering the layer of leaves on top of the car, Conner had to wonder how long the car and the victim had remained undiscovered. He looked back up the hillside, trying to gauge if the car could be seen as someone drove past. It was unlikely unless someone spotted the broken vegetation and got curious. That the car had been dark gray would've made it even harder to see, especially after sunset. Hopefully the coroner would be able to give them some idea of the time frame. At least that would give the investigating officers a place to start.

The state patrol officer said something to the detective before walking away. Conner hung back until Galloway waved him over. "Thanks for coming. I may have dragged you out here for nothing, but there's a chance we might have gotten our first break in the case. If so, I thought you'd want to get in on the ground level."

"I appreciate it."

They both turned to watch two men manhandling a stretcher down the hillside. It didn't take long for them to gently secure the body on it and start back up to the road above. Conner turned his attention toward the wrecked car. "How did anyone spot this in the first place?"

Galloway shook his head. "Pure dumb luck. A couple of teenagers were hiking down below when one of them fell and twisted his ankle. His buddy made him a makeshift crutch from a tree limb and then mostly dragged him up the hillside, hoping to reach the road where they could call for help or maybe stop a passing driver. If they hadn't happened to come up at this exact spot, they likely would've missed seeing the car at all. Poor kids."

"Where are they now?"

"They were transported to the nearest hospital to get the ankle X-rayed. They were both pretty shaken up by what they found, so the EMTs thought the two of them should both get checked out. The responding officer took their preliminary statements, but I can follow up with them later if it becomes necessary."

Conner felt bad for them. Even knowing their discovery would help bring closure to the victim's family, it would likely be a tough go for a while. He hoped they'd get counseling if they had trouble dealing with everything.

"Have they identified the victim?"

"Not yet." Galloway pulled out his notebook and glanced at his notes. "We ran the plates, but they don't match the car. Apparently, they were reported stolen over near Seattle. Thanks to the fire, we'll have to wait until they get the car to the lab to see if they can pull the vehicle identification number. Nothing in the glove compartment that helps, and the luggage burned."

He pointed toward the body. "We got his wallet, but the ID appears to be fake. Maybe fingerprints and DNA will tell us something."

Since they had no idea who the guy was at this point, there had to be something else going on that made Galloway think this was somehow tied to Mia. "Did he die from the impact?"

"Considering the severity of the impact, he might have eventually. The airbag deployed, which might be why he lived long enough to crawl out of the car."

Again, none of that made this anything but a tragic accident. "So why did they call you in?"

If anything, Galloway looked even more grim. "For starters, he also took a bullet to the chest. The coroner and the lab folks will have to work their magic to determine if he was shot first and that caused the accident or if someone finished him off afterward. Hopefully they'll be able to run ballistics. Last I checked, they were still looking for the bullet."

They both lapsed into silence while Conner digested that much. "So what ties all of this to Mia?"

"Maybe nothing. I had asked a few people in our office and some friends at the local state patrol headquarters to keep an eye out for anything that popped up that might involve a child."

He pointed toward the car. "There's no sign a kid was in the car at the time of the accident even though there's one of those booster things in the back seat. That alone is too much of a stretch to connect this to Mia, but we're pretty sure the vehicle matches one seen in the security video we got from the hospital."

The scenario was grim no matter how they looked at it. "So you're thinking there's a possibility that whoever the driver was, he might have dropped Mia off at the hospital and then ended up here."

Galloway nodded. "That's the theory, but right now it's mostly guesswork. It would certainly explain why no one has come looking for the little girl. He might have left her where he hoped she'd be kept safe and intended to come back for her when the coast was clear. Of course, even if that's how it played out, it doesn't explain why no one else is looking for her. Or him, for that matter."

A cold chill washed over Conner as the image of that broken flowerpot on Jody's patio flashed through his mind, not to mention the attack on the caseworker. Maybe someone was looking for Mia after all. He didn't bother pointing that out to Galloway. The man wouldn't have gotten to be a homicide detective if he wasn't smart with a talent for solving puzzles.

"So what's next?"

"We check the footage from the night Mia was left at the hospital to verify this is the car. If so, we'll know who dropped her off even if we don't know why. Otherwise, we'll be right back where we were— a lost kid and nothing to go on."

Galloway rolled his shoulders as if he needed to shake off some of the burden he carried every day from the job. They both knew some cases ended up with something to celebrate even if it was simply knowing justice had been done. Others came with no happy endings. After a bit, Galloway continued. "Meanwhile, they'll run his fingerprints and DNA. With luck, one or the other will give us a solid identification on him. They'll also see if they can get fingerprints or maybe even recover usable DNA from the booster seat and see if it matches Mia's. Considering the fire, that might not be possible."

So many ifs and maybes, but it was more than they had before this. "Is there anything I can do to help?"

Galloway gave him a considering look. "I'm guessing you're still keeping a close eye on your neighbor and her house."

Conner hoped he wasn't blushing. "I check in with Jody when I can. Whatever she heard the other night shook her up pretty badly. It would've helped if we could've given her a definitive answer about what happened that night. I talked to her yesterday, and she hasn't noticed anything else that worried her."

Actually, it wasn't yesterday, but closer to three o'clock that morning. The detective didn't need to know that. "She has my direct number and Deputy Stark's as well, so she can get in touch with one of us if she needs to."

"That's good. I'm going to head back to the office when they finish up here and start checking the footage. As soon as I learn anything definitive, I'll call."

"Same here." Conner checked the time. "I'm due out on patrol. Thanks for calling me in on this. I appreciate it."

Then he made his way up the hillside. Before getting into his car, he stopped to study the road leading up to where the car had veered off into the trees. How fast had that guy been driving? Some of the trees that had been damaged were far bigger than mere saplings. There also weren't any skid marks on the surface of the road indicating he'd slammed on the brakes trying to regain control of the vehicle. He was sure the investigative team would make note of that, too. The lab people were geniuses when it came to reconstructing the events that led up to an accident.

From the way things were adding up, this hadn't actually been an accident at all. Someone had come after the victim with deadly intent. Had that person given any thought at all to whether Mia was in the car? Of course, it could have been a random act of violence, but that didn't seem likely. Going with the assumption that the driver had some connection to Mia, it would've taken a cold-blooded killer to send both the driver and an innocent child careening out of control like that.

And that person was still out there somewhere. Conner straightened his shoulders and stiffened his resolve to keep Jody and Mia safe from harm. As he drove away, he offered up a prayer for guidance and asked that God watch over them when Conner couldn't be there to do it himself.

"Let's get your shoes on, little one. We have errands to run."

Mia looked up long enough to frown at Jody and then went right back to coloring. Praying for patience, Jody tried again, this time sounding firm. "Now, Mia. I need to put gas in the car, stop at the drugstore and do some grocery shopping. None of it will take us very long, and you can come back to finish coloring your picture."

Acting much put-upon, Mia carefully put her crayons back in the box, taking her own sweet time. Not quite defiant, but making her opinion on the planned outing all too clear. Finally, she put on her tennis shoes and waited impatiently for Jody to tie them for her.

"I know this isn't a fun outing, but we're out of milk, bread and juice boxes."

A few minutes later, Jody stepped out onto the porch and locked the door after Mia followed her outside. The two of them had settled into a pretty good routine, but she was amazed how much longer even simple errands took when a child was thrown into the mix. Not that she was complaining. Well, much, anyway.

As they headed toward the car, Mia stopped to study Conner's house. His car was in the driveway, so he was home. They hadn't seen him or Mutt for a couple of days, not since the day he'd been called in to work early. He hadn't actually said what kind of case they needed his help with, but there had been something in his eyes that made her think that it was a bad one. Of course, that could be her overactive imagination at work.

"Mutt and Deputy Dunne are probably still asleep." The man seemed to work a lot of extra hours. That's why she still hadn't mentioned their possible outing with Conner after church on Sunday in case he couldn't make it. There was no use in getting Mia all excited only to be disappointed if his job interfered.

She gave Mia a little nudge to get her moving again. "Maybe we'll see them later."

No sooner had she said the words than Conner's garage door opened and the man himself stepped into sight carrying a bucket. Mutt followed along right at his heels, which immediately spurred Mia into action. Before Jody could stop her, the little rascal was off and running, circling around the low hedge between their yards.

Mutt met her halfway and accepted Mia's hugs while wagging his tail, his tongue hanging out in a doggy grin. Conner looked as exasperated with the dog as she was with Mia. It was time to herd her back toward the car.

"Hi, Conner. Sorry, but she got away from me."

"And Mutt knows better than to go charging off like that." Then he grinned at her. "I suspect we're fighting a losing battle when it comes to those two."

"Probably. We need to run errands, and she's not too excited about the prospect. I swear that it takes more time to get her in and out of the car at each stop than the actual shopping does."

He continued to watch Mia and Mutt for a few seconds. "I'm going to wash my car, so I'll be out here for a while. Not to mention any names, but I wouldn't mind keeping an eye on someone for you. The unnamed person would probably be quite happy to spend time with her furry bestie."

Boy, that was tempting. While she was the one responsible for Mia, surely no one would question her leaving the little girl with Conner for an hour or so.

"If you're sure…"

"I'm okay with it if she is."

Jody walked over Conner's yard and knelt on one knee to get down to Mia's eye level. "Mia, you need to wait until you have permission to come over here. I know you'll remember next time. Now, Deputy Dunne has offered to let you hang out with him and Mutt while I run my errands. Would you like to do that?"

Mia gave her an emphatic nod and then once again wrapped her arm around Mutt's neck. "I'll be back in about an hour. Please behave for Deputy Dunne and do what he says, okay?"

Another nod and then Mia was off and running in circles around the yard while Mutt kept pace with her. Conner chuckled. "Where does she get the energy?"

"I think she steals it from me, which is why she never slows down while I'm tired most of the time. I'll get back as soon as I can."

"No rush. If she gets tired of chasing Mutt, I'll put her to work washing my wheels. If we finish with the car before you return, I'll turn them loose in the backyard. In fact, I was going to give Mutt a good brushing. Maybe I can get Mia to do it for me."

"She'd love that."

As she drove away, Conner squatted down beside Mia and demonstrated how to use a scrub brush on the wheels. No doubt both man and his little assistant would need dry clothes by the time they were done washing the car, but she'd bet they'd enjoy every minute.

The lines at the grocery store had been longer than Jody had expected, but she was finally on her way back home. Conner had been nice enough to text her a few minutes ago to let her know that they were out back enjoying cold drinks and apple slices dipped in peanut butter. He was going to spoil Mia, but it wasn't as if she wasn't guilty of doing a little of that herself.

The two-lane highway was clear of traffic, so Jody was making good time on her way back to their neighborhood. After retrieving Mia from Conner's house, she'd see if she could coax her into taking a nap. If she was successful, she might also stretch out and doze for a while.

Afterward, she'd put together a casserole for their dinner. Maybe inviting Conner and Mutt to join them would be a nice way to thank him for entertaining Mia. With that in mind, she'd also stopped at the local bakery to pick up one of their fresh-baked pies.

The sound of a revving engine broke through her train of thought. Glancing into the rearview mirror, she spotted a huge SUV coming up behind her at an alarming speed and closing fast. She pumped her brakes twice to flash the lights, hoping the driver would realize that he or she was exceeding the posted speed limit. Her warning had no effect. What were they thinking? If they wanted to pass her, now wasn't the time. Three cars had just appeared from around the corner ahead in the oncoming lane.

Jody gripped the steering wheel with all her strength, as if that would give her some control over the dangerous situation. What she needed was an escape route, but the shoulder was narrow before dropping off into a drainage ditch. She might have to chance it, though, if the reckless driver didn't slow down in a hurry.

Seeing the grille of the SUV up close and personal in her rearview mirror was beyond scary. At the last second, she spotted what looked like a dirt road coming up fast on her right. Taking a deep breath, she hit the brakes and jerked the steering wheel to the right to turn down the slight slope. She was vaguely aware of the SUV as it whizzed past, barely missing the back of her car in the process. It took all Jody's focus to keep her own vehicle under control as it bounced along on the badly rutted surface of the narrow road.

And when Jody's car finally rolled to a stop, all she could do was sit there and shake.

TEN

When Conner heard Jody pull into her driveway, he expected she would head straight over to pick up the munchkin. Maybe she was carrying her groceries inside before heading their way. When the delay stretched closer to twenty minutes, he knew something was wrong. There was no way Jody would leave Mia with him any longer than necessary.

Not that he minded hanging out with the little girl. She hadn't been any trouble, and Mutt was soaking up all the extra attention like a sponge. It had been funny watching her scrub the tires on Conner's car with such determination, even if she'd still missed a few spots along the way. She'd shown the same dedicated effort when she'd taken over brushing Mutt after Conner had given her a few pointers on what the dog liked. Right now Mutt was dozing in the shade with Mia stretched out right beside him.

"Mia, I think Jody might be back. Stay here with Mutt while I go check. Wave or nod if you understand."

When she lifted her hand in response, he added, "I won't be gone long. Like I said, stay here with Mutt."

He forced himself to walk calmly over to the gate, waiting until it clicked shut behind him before jogging down his driveway and over to Jody's. The trunk of her car was open and still held three canvas bags of groceries. He grabbed them on his way past and headed for her front porch. After shifting all the bags to one hand, he knocked and then opened the front door without waiting for a response.

"Jody, it's Conner. I've got the rest of your groceries."

She sat motionless at her kitchen table and didn't respond to his greeting, which only increased his concern. He cautiously made his way across the living room to the kitchen, not wanting to startle her. She finally looked up when he set the bags on the table. Her face was blotchy, and her eyes were red and swollen.

"Are you okay?"

Her eyes brimmed full with a new crop of tears as she shook her head. Conner immediately closed the remaining distance between them, doing a visual inventory to see if she was hurt. No bumps or bruises that he could see. Thinking back, he didn't remember seeing any obvious damage to her car, but something bad had happened. Finally, he eased her up off the chair and wrapped his arms around her.

"What happened, Jody?"

She buried her face against his chest, her tears

burning hot as they soaked into his T-shirt. He gently stroked her back and let her cry it out. Finally, she sniffled a few times and then pulled back a little. Touching the damp spot on his shirt, she whispered, "Sorry I got your shirt wet."

He struggled to maintain a calm facade. "Jody, I'm not worried about my shirt. I'm worried about what has you so upset."

"Someone ran me off the road on my way home from the store. It was one of those huge SUVs, and I thought it was going to plow right into me. By some miracle, I managed to turn off onto a farm road right before we would've collided."

His breath caught in his chest. Jody wasn't the kind to exaggerate or overreact. If she said it had been a close call, he believed her. "Were you able to get any kind of description of the vehicle other than it was an SUV?"

"It was gray or maybe dark silver."

Unfortunately, gray was almost as common as white when it came to popular car colors. "No make or model?"

She shook her head. "It all happened so fast. I heard an engine revving, like it was speeding up. When I looked in my rearview mirror, all I saw was this huge car coming straight at me fast. At first, I thought they were speeding up to pass me, but there were cars in the oncoming lane."

"What happened after you turned off the road?"

"I fought hard to keep control of my car, since

I had to take the turn way too fast. It was a gravel road with real deep ruts. Luckily, I stopped just shy of hitting a huge boulder. Afterward, I sat there until I could stop shaking enough to drive back home."

When another tear trickled down her cheek, he wiped it away with his fingertip and then pulled her in close again. She wrapped her arms around him, her fingers grabbing hold of the back of his shirt. "You did good, Jody. You didn't panic and made sure you were okay to drive before getting back out on the road."

He knew she'd turned the corner when she drew a sharp breath. "Where's Mia?"

"She's in my backyard with Mutt. I was worried something was wrong when you didn't come get her right after you got back. She promised she'd stay with him until I returned for her." He reluctantly released his hold on her and took half a step back to give each of them a little breathing space. "I'll go get her now if you want."

"Yes, please."

He gave in to a powerful temptation to touch her soft cheek one more time. "While I'm gone, you might want to go splash some cold water on your face."

Jody bravely offered him a crooked smile. "I look that bad, do I?"

He grinned at her. "Do you really think I'm stupid enough to give you an honest answer to that question?"

Although, tears and all, he still thought she was

beautiful. There was something about those dark eyes and sweet smile that ticked off all the right boxes for him. Considering what she'd been through, this wasn't the time or the place. He retreated to a safer distance. "I'll be back in a few minutes. I need to lock up the house before we head over here."

He was out the door and running back to check on Mia and Mutt. As soon as he stepped through the gate into his backyard, he breathed a sigh of relief and waited for his pulse to return to normal. No use in scaring the little girl or upsetting the dog. Jody was fine, and Mia was safe—at least for the moment.

The image Jody had painted of her encounter with that SUV had left him badly shaken. He might be jumping to conclusions, but he didn't think so. Jody had been lucky to survive what sounded like a deliberate attack. Even if it had been done on the spur of the moment, he had no doubt the goal had been to run her off the road. Only dumb luck and Jody's quick thinking had saved her from getting badly hurt if not killed.

He didn't think Jody was thinking along those lines, but she didn't know about the accident scene he'd visited with Detective Galloway. Someone had sent that car tumbling down that hillside, either by running it off the road or by shooting the driver and causing him to lose control of the vehicle. It seemed to be too much of a coincidence that someone had tried something similar today with Jody.

He studied Mia, who was still curled up next to

Mutt. His gut said that somehow it all circled back to her. They needed to keep her safe until they figured out what was going on. With that in mind, he dialed Galloway's number to fill him in on the situation. There was nothing either of them could do about what had happened, but the man needed to be kept in the loop.

After giving him a succinct summary of the events, Conner asked, "Am I reading too much into this?"

"No, you're not. As soon as I hang up, I'll go rattle some cages and see if I can hurry things along. I know you can't park yourself at Ms. Kruse's house 24-7, but do what you can. I sure wish that kid could tell us what's going on."

Conner stared at the little girl in question, his heart aching for her, his resolve to keep her safe solidifying. "Me, too, Detective. Me, too."

The day after her scary adventure, Jody hurt from head to toe and back again. Even though her car hadn't actually hit anything, she'd sustained a good-size bruise on her chest from the shoulder harness. She suspected her other aches and pains had resulted from the tension in her muscles as she'd fought to control the car as it bounced along the ruts in the gravel road. No matter what the cause, aspirin and two hot baths had finely taken the edge off the pain. Sadly, nothing was helping her get past the few minutes when she'd really thought she was going to die.

She'd spent a lot of time thanking God that He'd somehow guided her to safety.

She also thanked Him for bringing Conner into her life. After her almost accident, he'd really stepped up to help. Not only had he stayed for dinner that night, he'd cooked it. He'd even let Mia help. If Jody hadn't been hurting so badly at the time, she would've been snapping picture after picture of the cuteness of it all.

Afterward, he'd also insisted on doing the dishes, once again soliciting Mia's help. The little girl had carefully dried the few unbreakable things that Conner had handed her before setting them on the table. The entire time, Mutt sat beside Jody, his huge head in her lap. Stroking his soft fur helped soothe her badly shaken nerves.

At least the past two days had been uneventful. For the most part, she and Mia stayed home and spent time working in the yard and doing a few chores around the house. Yesterday had been the first time Jody ventured out driving, when she'd taken Mia to see her counselor again. Dr. Mayberry had gotten Mia to draw a couple of pictures for her, but they didn't reveal any huge secrets or offer up any information about Mia's family. Like Jody, the doctor remained concerned about Mia's refusal to talk, but she also thought it was promising that Mia now slept through the night far more often.

Now it was a bright and sunny Sunday morning, and she and Mia were on their way to church again.

She still hadn't told Mia that they might be going out to brunch after the service with Conner. His car wasn't in his driveway, but she didn't know if he'd already left for church or if he hadn't gotten home from work yet. They'd find out soon enough.

Assuming Conner usually sat in the same area, she led Mia down the side aisle of the church. The pew where he'd sat the last time was empty. She couldn't help but be disappointed, but he'd warned her that sometimes his job interfered. Evidently Mia had expected him to be there, too, because she was frowning as she scoped out the sanctuary.

"If you're looking for Conner, he warned me that he might have to work. I know he really hoped to be here with us."

The music was starting, so Jody nudged Mia forward. "It's time to sit down."

As soon as they were settled, Mia leaned forward to pluck one of the hymnals out of the holder in front of them. When Jody tried to take it, intending to open it to the right page, Mia wouldn't let her. Then she pointed toward another hymnal, a clear hint that she wasn't going to share hers with anyone other than Conner. Now wasn't the time for a discussion about manners and how things were done at church.

The choir was beginning the second verse of the opening hymn when Mia snuggled in closer to Jody to make room for someone else. Conner met her gaze over Mia's head. "Sorry I'm late. I had to stop back by the office on the way here."

Meanwhile, Mia shoved her hymnal into Conner's hands. He smiled down at her and opened the book to the right page and then supported one side of the book while Mia held the other. Now that the little rascal had everything and everyone arranged to her liking, she was far happier. Jody couldn't blame her. More and more, spending time with Conner felt good, felt right.

Only time would tell if the special connection she felt for him was because of their mutual concern for Mia or if it was something more, something special between them. Before she could decipher exactly how she felt about that, Jody turned her attention to Pastor Dahl's sermon. As always, his gentle presence and the words of God that he shared with them all helped to wash away the trials of the past week and brought her peace.

After the service, she followed Conner to the diner again, where she parked her car next to his. He opened the back passenger door and unbuckled Mia from her booster seat. The little minx held up her arms, demanding to be picked up. He did so effortlessly and waited for Jody to join them before heading into the diner. Once again, there were several officers in uniform scattered around the place. After waving at Conner, they studied her and Mia, making no effort to hide their obvious curiosity.

Conner headed for a booth in the far corner, where he set Mia on one bench and took a seat on the opposite side while Jody slid in next to Mia. The two adults studied the menu as Mia reached for the small box of crayons the server had left for her and began coloring the pictures on the children's menu.

After a server swung by to take their orders, Jody smiled across at Conner. "I'm glad you could make it this morning. I really enjoyed Pastor Dahl's sermon. I always do, but today's seemed to be extra good."

"I thought so, too." He added cream and sugar to his coffee. "I tried several churches after I moved here, but I knew I'd found the right place for me the first time I heard him preach. There's something about the way he explains things that I really like."

"I felt the same way when I first met him."

He sipped the coffee and set it back down. "We haven't had a chance to talk the past couple of days. How are you doing?"

"Mostly fine. A little twitchy when a car comes up behind me, but I figure that'll pass eventually."

"I'm sure it will. It's a common aftereffect when people are involved in an accident, or even if they had a narrow escape like you did. I usually try to warn people what to expect so they don't think they're the only one who has ever felt that way."

That was nice of him. It occurred to her that Conner already knew that she loved being a teacher, but she'd never asked him much about his job. Maybe it was time to start. "How about you? Has it been a busy week at work?"

He shrugged. "It had its moments. Some evenings are quiet. Other times you can't catch your breath."

"If I'm not being too nosy, why did you choose law enforcement for a career? Does it run in your family like you hear about in television shows?"

"I guess that's true in some cases, but not in mine. My father was a plumber, and my mother was a homemaker. I'm not sure what they would make of me being a cop."

"They don't know?"

The brief flash of pain that crossed his face told her the answer without him saying a single word. She hastened to apologize. "I'm sorry, Conner. I didn't mean to bring up a difficult subject."

"That's okay. They died twenty years ago when I was ten. A drunk driver hit their car." He toyed with the salt and pepper shakers on the table, not meeting her gaze. "I suspect that's why I was drawn into law enforcement. You know, to do what I can to make sure the same thing doesn't happen to some other kid's parents, not to mention putting bad guys in jail. My folks were more into turning the other cheek, so I'm not sure what they would've thought of me being a cop."

Jody reached across the table to lay her hand on top of his. He'd been about to switch the positions of the salt and pepper shakers for the fourth time. Sensing he was uncomfortable with the conversation, she quietly said, "You do more than go after the bad guys. You also help take care of the innocents."

She glanced at Mia to emphasize the point and

then turned back to him. "I think they'd be very proud of how their son turned out."

His eyes had been focused on their hands, but he slowly looked up to meet her gaze. "I've always hoped so. Grandpa Jasper was part of my decision, too. He took me in after they died. It wasn't easy for him, but he never complained. Not once."

He sounded confused by that. She couldn't help but wonder why. In a perfect world, family took care of family, and obviously that's what his grandfather had done. In her case, she'd had to find a new family for herself. Like Conner, she'd been lucky to land in a good place.

Their food arrived, ending the conversation. After that, they kept things light and fun. She insisted on paying the bill since Conner had treated them the last time. On the way out, she realized that she could get used to hanging out with Conner and Mia—like they were more than friends with a common purpose to keep the little girl safe.

She now shared the same risk as Mia of getting too attached to Conner and Mutt. It would really hurt when the little girl returned to her family. But when that happened, it might hurt just as much if Conner reverted to his earlier stance that keeping watch over the two of them had been simply a part of his job, nothing more. Once Mia was gone from Jody's life, Conner might be as well. But that was a problem for another day. Right now, she would enjoy their time together.

ELEVEN

On Tuesday morning, Jody and Mia made good time driving over Stevens Pass. Traffic had been remarkably light on Highway 2 all the way to the interstate that took them south into Seattle. They were on their way to have lunch with the Burks, the couple who had fostered Jody back when she'd needed a safe harbor. Since she'd moved east of the mountains after college, they mainly kept in touch with long phone calls every couple of weeks, usually on Sunday evenings. It was always good to chat with them, but it would be nice to see them in person again.

Mia had been looking at her favorite picture book, the one with a German shepherd on the cover, but she tossed it aside and let out a huge sigh. It appeared that long car rides weren't her thing.

Jody caught her attention in the rearview mirror. "I think you'll really like Mama and Papa Burks. They let me come stay with them when I was about nine years older than you are now. I ended up living with them until I graduated from college and became a teacher."

None of that seemed to interest Mia in the least, so Jody brought out the big guns. "They have a dog named Bessie."

The little girl's eyes lit up as she reached for the picture book she'd dropped on the car seat. She held it up so Jody could see the cover and pointed to the Mutt look-alike on the front. Jody shook her head. "Nope, Bessie doesn't look anything like Mutt. She's a bulldog. Have you ever seen one?"

A head shake was Mia's only answer.

"Well, she's a real sweetie, and she loves cuddles as much as Mutt does."

Mia held up her hand with her fingers pressed together and then pretended to eat something. "Yes, Bessie loves treats. I'm sure Mama Burks will have some on hand that you can give her."

The brief conversation kept them both entertained long enough to reach their destination. Mama Burks must have been watching for them, because the front door swung open before Jody had a chance to knock.

"Come in, come in."

As soon as they made it through the door, Jody was enfolded in a huge hug that felt like coming home. Jody pressed a kiss on the older woman's cheek and then took a step back. "Thanks for inviting us today. I'd like you to meet Mia."

Mama Burks knew kids in foster care could be skittish when it came to meeting new people. Rather than trying to hug Mia, she took a step back and smiled down at her. "I'm awfully glad to meet you, Mia. Jody here has told me all about you. She says you're a big help in the kitchen. Maybe you could give me a hand when it comes time to set the table for lunch."

Mia looked to Jody for her input before answering. When Jody nodded, Mia did, too.

Jody looked around. Normally, her foster father would come charging from wherever he was in the house to greet her. "Where's Papa?"

"In the family room with Bessie. He wants to take her for a walk before lunch."

It was no surprise when Mia's eyes lit up at the mention of the dog. Jody took her hand again. "Come on, little one. I'll introduce you to Bessie and Papa Burks. Maybe he'll let you help him take Bessie for a walk. She doesn't walk as fast or as far as Mutt, but I bet you'd enjoy getting some exercise after that long car ride."

The three of them walked into the family room, where Papa Burks was fitting Bessie with her harness. The bulldog perked up when she spotted Mia and waddled toward her, offering a huge snort by way of a greeting.

Mia laughed and immediately reached out to pat Bessie's wrinkly forehead and then cautiously scratched the dog's back. The dog wiggled with delight and clearly wanted more of the same. She spun around and sat down to afford her new friend easier access. When Mia hit a particularly itchy spot, Bessie rumbled in pleasure. Mia grinned and started using both hands to make sure she did a thorough job.

All three adults watched the dog and little girl with big smiles on their faces. After a few seconds, Papa Burks wrapped his arm around Jody's shoulders and gave her a quick hug. "It's pretty clear who rules the roost around here. Bessie will sit there as long as Mia is willing to pet her."

"In that case, we may never leave this room. Mia really loves dogs."

"I was about to take Bessie out for a while. Do you think Mia would be comfortable going with us?"

Jody left it up to the little girl. "Mia, would you like to stay here with me or go on a walk with Bessie and Papa Burks?"

Papa Burks joined the conversation. "Bessie is getting older and doesn't like to go very far. We only go around the block, which takes about twenty minutes. I'm sure Bessie would like to show you around the neighborhood. What do you say?"

Mia stared up at Papa Burks for a few seconds before slowly nodding. Then she held up her hand with the fingers pressed together again. He frowned and apologized. "I'm sorry, honey, I don't understand."

Jody translated. "My neighbor has a retired police dog named Mutt. Deputy Dunne taught Mia to hold a treat in her hand like that and then wait until Mutt sits down before giving it to him. She's asking if you have any treats she can give Bessie."

Mama Burks headed for the kitchen. "I'll put a few in a plastic bag for you, Mia. I'll be right back."

At the same time, Papa snapped Bessie's leash onto her harness. "Would you like to hold the leash, Mia?"

Jody loved the determined look on Mia's face as she reached for the loop on the leash and took it in a firm grip. The three of them waited by the front door for Mama to return with the treats.

Papa gave Jody's shoulder a soft squeeze. "Don't worry about us. We won't be gone long, and I've got my phone with me. I can call if someone gets worried about being away from you too long."

"I appreciate that." Jody gave Papa another hug and then patted Mia on the head. "I'll stay right here to help Mama Burks. If you get worried, point to his phone. He'll call me, and I'll come running."

Mia was far more interested in getting out the door with the dog than she was in knowing what Jody would be doing while she was gone. Jody watched until the trio reached the end of the street before joining Mama in the kitchen, who pointed toward the counter by the sink. She'd set out salad makings along with a chef's knife and a vegetable peeler. It felt like old times with Jody putting together a tossed salad while Mama made sandwiches for lunch.

"I hope Mia likes grilled cheese sandwiches."

"She does."

Mama wiped her hands on a towel and turned to face Jody. "So, while they're gone, I want to know

how you're doing. It can't be easy taking care of someone who doesn't talk."

Mama wasn't being critical, but Jody still felt like
she needed to defend Mia. "She manages to com-
municate remarkably well even without words. The
counselor she's been seeing feels certain that Mia
will eventually start talking again. I can already see
a huge difference in her in the time that she's been
with me."

Mama smiled up at her. "That doesn't surprise me
in the least, Jody. You have a kind heart, and kids
can sense that. I take it that the police still haven't
figured out where she came from or where her family might be."

"Not so far."

Jody began peeling the carrots as she debated how
much of what had been happening she should share.
As much as she loved and trusted the Burkses, she
wasn't sure Conner and Detective Galloway would
want her to go blabbing about the investigation. Besides, knowing about the attempted break-in and how
Jody had been run off the road would only worry the
older couple. Papa had a heart condition, and she
didn't want to stress him unnecessarily.

Mama had been buttering slices of bread for the
grilled cheese sandwiches, but she set the knife down
for a minute. "I'm guessing there's something you
either can't or don't want to tell me. That's fine, but
promise me if you need help that you'll ask for it. If
not from us, then from the police or the caseworker.

Taking care of someone like Mia should be a group effort even if you're the one who has primary custody of her for now. We've been praying for you, Mia and her family every day."

Knowing Jody had their support meant everything. "I appreciate that. If I do half as well caring for Mia as you did taking care of me, I'll be satisfied. I've also asked and received help from both the police and Mia's caseworker."

Mama went back to buttering the bread. "Are you talking about the police in general or the deputy who lives next door to you?"

There was a suspicious note in Mama's voice. What was she thinking? Worse yet, what had Jody revealed without even realizing it? Choosing her words carefully, she said, "Both, actually. The detective in charge of Mia's case touches base with me when he can. Deputy Dunne has been very patient with Mia, who really loves his dog. Actually, it's a case of mutual admiration. There was one time Mia and I were working in the backyard when she heard Mutt on the other side of the fence. She found a knothole in one of the cedar boards and used it to spy on him and his owner."

Smiling, she let the memory play out in her head. "My fence is six feet high, so imagine my shock when Mutt came flying over it to spend time with Mia."

"How did his owner respond to that?"

Jody chuckled. "Not at all well. It was a major infraction in the dog's training. Conner was really nice but firm with both Mia and Mutt. He explained to Mia that the dog has rules he has to follow."

"You like him. I'm talking about Deputy Dunne, not the dog."

There was no point in denying it. Mama knew her too well. "I have a lot of respect for him, as well. He's a great guy and has been really good with Mia. I get the feeling that it's a big part of his nature to protect those he feels responsible for. Considering he's a deputy sheriff, a whole lot of people fall under that umbrella. It's a hard job, and one he takes really seriously."

She smiled again. "I don't think he's spent much time around kids, but he's a natural. He explains things in ways she understands. When she drew a picture of him and Mutt, she showed him that it should go on his refrigerator like the one we put on ours. He asked if it was okay to hang it with tape because he didn't have any magnets."

Her foster mother nodded with approval. "Thereby showing her that her opinion matters to him. That's important with all kids, but especially when it comes to ones who are going through a rough patch."

Mama started stacking slices of cheese on the bread. "While I'm glad he's so good with Mia, I'm more curious about how he is with you."

Then she gave Jody one of those mom looks that said very clearly that nothing less than the truth would do. "I really like him, and I think he likes me as well. I suspect my feelings for him could easily turn into something more, but it scares me. I'm not sure how much of what I'm feeling is due to the circumstances that have thrown us together. Besides, he's said on more than one occasion that he's only doing his job."

"But?"

"As it turns out, we've both been attending the same church but at different services. I started taking Mia to the early service, because there are fewer people and I didn't want people inviting her to Sunday school."

Mama set the tray of sandwiches next to the electric griddle on the counter. "Smart move. That way you don't have to explain about her not talking to the adults, but especially the other kids. It's better to wait until she's comfortable before putting her into too many new situations."

She paused to check on the pie she had in the oven. Evidently it was done, because she took it out and set it on a trivet to cool. "So what does attending the same church have to do with his job?"

"Well, if he's only doing his job, why would he invite the two of us out to eat after the service? He took us to a diner that's a local hangout for people in law enforcement. If he really wants to keep his personal life separate from his professional one, it seems strange that he'd take us to the one place where he'd be mixing the two together."

She set the salad on the table as she waited for

Mama to respond. It didn't take long. "Jody, what I'm about to say is based solely on what you've told me, which isn't much. I know you're not telling me everything, probably because you don't think it's your story to tell. However, I'd say his mind is telling him to stick to his job, but his heart is wanting something more."

That assessment sent Jody's pulse skyrocketing. Could Conner be feeling the same confusing mix of emotions that she was? When he'd held her so carefully after she'd been run off the road, it had felt so right to turn to him for comfort.

The front door opened, derailing any further chance of continuing the conversation. It was probably for the best. It would be hard to tell Mama Burks any more about her interactions with Conner without confessing everything that had happened since Mia had come to stay with her. She didn't want to worry either of the Burkses, especially when there wasn't anything they could do to help from the other side of the mountains.

Mia came into the kitchen still holding on to Bessie's leash and dragging the tired dog along behind her. After letting Jody hug her, Mia held up the empty treat bag to Mama. The older woman smiled down at her. "Boy, Bessie must have been really well-behaved on the walk to have earned that many treats."

Bessie parked herself next to Mia as they both stared up at the empty bag. Mama knew exactly what both of them wanted, but she set the bag on the counter out of reach. "Maybe Bessie can have another treat before you and Jody have to leave, but too many aren't good for her. It would be like letting you live on nothing but cookies."

Papa joined the crowd. "Mia, can you unfasten Bessie's leash? I'm thinking she's going to need a nap after her walk."

Then he winked at Jody. "She's not the only one."

His wife rolled her eyes. "He and Bessie spend a lot more time napping together than walking together. His doctor and her vet both say they need to reverse that ratio."

Before Papa could come up with a retort, she made a shooing motion with her hands. "Mia, after you help Bessie with her leash, please wash your hands, because we're about to eat lunch. We're having salad and grilled cheese sandwiches." She paused to give her husband a pointed look. "There will be peach pie with a big scoop of ice cream for anyone who eats all of their vegetables."

Mia unsnapped Bessie's leash and handed it to Papa Burks. That done, she went over to check Bessie's water bowl. Seeing it was less than half-full, she carried it over and stood in front of the sink. When she started to set it back down on the floor, Jody realized Mia was intending to pull a chair over to the counter so she could reach the faucet. She immediately volunteered to help. "I'll fill it for you this time."

Accepting the now-full bowl, Mia carried it back

over to where she'd found it and gently set it down, only spilling a little bit on the way. Bessie rewarded her efforts by immediately shoving her face into the bowl and lapping up about half of its contents. When she lifted her head, rivulets of water dripped out of her jowls onto the floor, which Mia thought was really funny. Jody handed her the special towel that the Burkses kept in a handy spot for such moments. Then she used a stage whisper to share a family truth. "Bulldogs are messy, but we love them anyway. And you know what? I think that God feels that same way about all of His children." After a second's consideration, Mia gave her a solemn nod and then scrubbed the floor dry.

TWELVE

It felt like cheating, but Jody picked up an extra-large take-and-bake pizza for dinner on the way home from the Burkses'. It wasn't as if she didn't have something at home she could cook for her and Mia. But after driving so much of the day, she didn't have the energy. A smaller pizza would've been plenty for the two of them. But on the off chance Conner was home, he might appreciate having an easy meal, too.

Sadly, his driveway was empty when they got home, so he must be working. Oh, well, having leftover pizza in the fridge for a snack or for lunch the next day was never a bad thing. She flipped on the lights in the living room and stood back to let Mia into the house.

"I don't know about you, but I'm not really hungry yet. Is it okay if we wait until we have a chance to get settled before we eat dinner?"

Mia nodded and flopped down on the couch. When she pointed at the television, Jody said, "I'll put the pizza away and then come back to find something for you to watch."

After making room in the fridge for the pizza box, she did what she'd been doing all too often since the night someone tried to break in. She turned on the patio lights to do a quick check on the backyard. It had become a habit she couldn't seem to shake.

Up until that minute, there had been no sign the intruder had been back. No broken pots, no crushed plants, no footprints. But this time, there was something else—something so much more frightening. The back door was open. It was only a fraction of an inch, but she knew she'd made sure it was closed and locked when they left that morning.

As a single woman living alone, she'd always been careful about such things. Now, after everything that had happened, it had become a compulsion. Backing away from the door, she picked up a rolling pin and headed into the living room. Mia was still waiting patiently for Jody to turn on the television.

"I'll be right back, Mia."

She took off down the hall to her own room and checked under the bed, in the closet and in the bathroom. Then she did the same in Mia's room and the guest room. Satisfied the house was empty except for the two of them, she stopped long enough to turn on one of Mia's favorite cartoon shows and then retreated to the kitchen to call Conner.

He answered on the first ring, his cop voice giving every word a sharp edge. "What's happened? Are you and Mia okay?"

The sound of his voice went a long way toward calming her nerves. "We're fine. We got home a few minutes ago after spending the day visiting my foster parents in Seattle. Everything in the house looks just like we left it, and there's no one in the house but us."

"That's the good news." She drew a shuddering breath. "Conner, the back door was unlocked and open about an inch when we got home."

"You locked it before you left."

It wasn't a question, but she affirmed his assumption anyway. "I did. Actually, I locked it before we went to bed last night and checked it again right before we left. I swear it was locked."

"Did you call it in?"

"No, mainly because there's no proof that anyone came inside the house at all. I didn't want to make you or another deputy come all the way here to look at nothing."

There was a long silence before he spoke again. "Okay, I was about to take my dinner break. Rather than grabbing a burger, I'll come there instead. If I find anything suspicious, we'll write up an official report. How does that sound?"

Relief made her knees weak enough that she pulled out a chair and sat down. "It sounds like it's a good thing I bought an extra-large pizza for dinner."

He laughed; she suspected it was mainly because

she needed him to. "Please tell me it's not an all-veggie pizza."

This time, she was the one who laughed. "No, caveman, you're safe. Pepperoni and sausage all the way."

"See you soon."

It had taken everything Conner had to remain calm on the phone with Jody. This stuff had to end. That wouldn't happen until they found the person who was terrorizing her and put them behind bars. The only question was how to catch a phantom. At least the time it had taken to reach their neighborhood had given him a chance to rein in his anger.

On impulse, he stopped by his own house first in order to bring Mutt over to Jody's with him. It would make both Mia and the dog happy to spend some time together while Conner talked to Jody. In fact, he should probably leave Mutt with them while he finished his shift. He couldn't stay long, and the dog's presence would help Jody feel safer.

She opened the door as soon as he stepped onto her porch. He released his hold on Mutt, who headed straight into the house to find his little friend. Without hesitation, Conner held out his arms and gathered Jody in close. It was probably unprofessional, but he didn't care. He was there on his own time and needed the contact as much as she did. "Are you really okay?"

"Better now that you're here. Thank you for coming."

"I can't stay long. But before I have to leave, Mutt and I will take a quick look around out back." He glanced inside through the front window and smiled. The dog was already snuggled up with Mia. "Well, if I can pry him away from Mia long enough to do a quick patrol."

"I'll put her to work setting the table while I serve up the pizza."

"Good plan."

First up, he checked the back door. There were a few small scratches, but nothing that normal wear and tear wouldn't cause. He snapped a few pictures with his phone to compare to the ones from the last time an intruder had tried to break in. All things considered, it was probably a good thing Jody had called him instead of the emergency number. Sheila might have believed Jody had double-checked the lock before she'd left for the day, but it was doubtful that any of the other deputies would've done more than a cursory check. Not that they wouldn't care, but they couldn't spend a lot of time on a case that offered next to nothing in the way of evidence.

He'd have to remind her to make sure anyone who responded to any future situations contacted Detective Galloway if Conner himself was unavailable. As soon as Mutt gave the area a good sniff, he went from Mia's cuddly buddy to a K-9 dog on the job. He wove a pattern across the patio and then across the grass with his nose to the ground. Whatever trail he followed led to almost the exact same spot along the back fence as the last time. That wasn't going to make Jody any happier than it did Conner.

When he went back inside, the smell of pepperoni and sausage scented the air. Mia was already at the table. It was no surprise that Mutt immediately circled around to sit next to her chair. Conner washed his hands at the kitchen sink and took what had somehow become his usual seat at the table. Jody set a glass of iced tea by his plate and another by her own, while Mia got milk.

When Jody sat down, Mia put the palms of her hands together and bowed her head. Jody smiled and then turned to him. "Would you like to say grace for us?"

Conner used the same simple prayer he had the first time Jody and Mia had asked him to say grace, but with one addition. "We thank You, Lord, for the food before us. Please watch over this household and keep those within safe from harm. Amen."

Mia immediately reached for her milk, but Jody looked stricken. Maybe he should've said that last part silently. God would've heard it anyway, and it wouldn't have scared Jody. Still, he had to tell her what he and Mutt had found, so she was bound to be upset anyway. She should also know that he believed her about the door having been locked when she left the house.

Now wasn't the time for that discussion. It could wait until they finished eating and Mia went back to watching her show.

"So how was your drive to Seattle?"

Jody followed his lead. "It was a perfect day to drive across the pass. I never get tired of the beauty of the Cascades. My foster parents were really glad to finally meet Mia. It had been a while since I'd made the trip over to see them, although we talk frequently. Their kids and I have all tried to explain how Zoom works, but Papa Burks isn't really into newfangled things like that."

Then she tipped her head in Mutt's direction. "And Mia made a new friend named Bessie."

Conner raised his eyebrows in mock surprise and directed his questions to Mia. "Really? Was she anything like Mutt?"

Mia glanced at Mutt and then shook her head. Then she puffed out her cheeks as she clenched her hands in fists and held her arms out to the side and bent forward at the elbows. It took him a second to decide she was trying to flex her muscles. "So Bessie has a fatter face and is more muscular?"

That earned him a nod. Then Mia snorted several times, sounding more like a pig than a dog. Finally, Jody took pity on him. "Bessie is an English bulldog."

Ah, now he understood what Mia had been trying to convey. "Did you like her?"

Mia looked to Jody as if hoping she would continue to speak for her. "She did like Bessie. She and my foster father took Bessie for a stroll around the block. The old girl is getting up there in doggy years, so that's about as far as she is interested in walking. When they got back, Mia made sure Bessie had a full bowl of water. If you've never seen how much water a bulldog can store in their jowls, it's amazing."

Mia giggled and made motions like something was falling from her cheeks. Again, Jody translated. "When Bessie finished drinking, about half the water dripped out of her jowls onto the floor. Mia was nice enough to clean up after her new friend. After that, Bessie took a long nap."

Mia followed that up by closing her eyes and snorting again. Conner met Jody's gaze, relieved to see her now looking amused instead of frightened. "I take it bulldogs snore, or at least Bessie does."

Mia nodded. Then she reached out to give Mutt a good scratching as if to remind him that he was her best buddy. That spending time with Bessie was a momentary fling.

Conner pointed at his own nose. "Mia, Mutt can probably smell her on you, but he doesn't mind that you spent time with another dog. He knows how much he means to you."

Even if that would cause problems when Mia returned to her family. The dog wasn't the only one who would hate the day the little girl disappeared from their lives. But until that happened, they still needed to keep her safe.

It didn't take long for Mia to finish her milk and pizza. When she and Mutt were stretched out on the living room floor watching cartoons, Conner finished off his own meal and checked the time. He had about five minutes before he needed to get back out on the road. "I'll make this short, Jody. There's not a lot of evidence that someone jimmied the lock on the door."

When she started to protest, he cut her off. "I didn't say there was no evidence. It's just a few scratches that I don't remember being there the last time. Having said that, if I hadn't had occasion to look at the lock closely before, I would've written the damage off to normal usage. Mutt did pick up a scent at the door and followed it out to the same area as the last time by the back fence. No crushed plants or anything that I could see."

"So you think someone was here."

"I think it's a strong possibility. I will let Detective Galloway know."

She started clearing the table. "So there's still nothing we can do."

He couldn't argue with her assessment, but at least he could share his plan. "For starters, I'm going to leave Mutt here while I finish my shift. I can either pick him up in the morning or stop by when I get off work. That will be somewhere between eleven thirty and midnight."

"Would he be okay here all night? I don't want to upset his routine if it would cause problems."

Good question. "He should be fine. If you could let him out in the backyard before you turn in for the night or walk him around on his leash out front, that would help. You can always text me if you think I should pick him up."

"Thanks."

She stopped what she was doing and faced him, her arms crossed around her waist as if protecting herself from a physical blow. "I'm afraid in my own home. I don't like it."

For the second time since he'd arrived, Conner found himself pulling Jody into his arms. "I don't like it, either. I promise I'll find a way to fix this."

There was a hint of confusion in her dark eyes as she stared into his for a heartbeat or two before she spoke. "Because it's your job?"

The question knocked him sideways, the answer so much more complicated than a simple yes or no. The county paid him to protect its citizens, and he took pride in doing his job to the best of his abilities. That said, he'd be lying to both her and himself if he denied that this case meant so much more.

When he didn't immediately answer, Jody struggled to free herself of his embrace. Instincts older than time warned him if he let her go now and put the shield of his job between them, he risked losing something special that he might never find again.

Instead, he rested his forehead against hers and shared his truth. "Yes, it's my job, Jody. But I think we both know this has become something more than that. I care about Mia, and I care about you. A lot. It's been a long time since I let anyone get this close. It's easier to sleep nights when I keep some emotional distance from the stuff I see every day."

She looked at him with such warm concern that it made it hard to draw a full breath. The clock was ticking, and he really should leave. That didn't mean he would walk away without finishing what he needed to say. "But it's too late to do that when it comes to you and Mia. I have to look at the facts of the case objectively, but every minute I spend in your company makes that harder and harder. I realize that I'm making a hash of this."

Jody put her finger across his lips, putting a stop to the flood of words flowing out of his mouth. "It's good to know that I'm not the only one who is confused here, but I think there are a few things we can agree on. Starting with that Mia's safety comes first."

She paused as if awaiting his response. As soon as he nodded, she continued. "The circumstances surrounding her situation threw us together in a way that would never have happened if she hadn't come to stay with me. Maybe we would have eventually become friends or even something more even without her presence jump-starting the process. We'll never know, since that's not how things happened."

Her fingertips brushed across his cheek, a simple touch that he felt in the depth of his heart. "Like I said, she has to be our first priority right now. When everything is said and done, you and I might remain just friends, or it could be something more. Either way, I'm glad God brought you into our lives right when we needed you the most."

It had been so long that he'd had someone in his life who was more than a coworker or a casual friend. All the words he wanted to say were so jumbled up inside him that he wasn't sure he'd make any sense if he tried to speak. Instead, he found another way to express himself.

He kissed her.

THIRTEEN

Jody wasn't sure which of them was more surprised by the kiss—her or Conner. It was probably a tie, considering her brain was totally scrambled, while he went from being right there in front of her to standing across the room before she even realized he was moving. She didn't know whether to laugh or cry.

"I've got to go, Jody." Then he frowned. "Not because of what just happened, but I'm on duty."

She managed to nod. "I know. I'll keep Mutt. If he seems unhappy, I'll let you know to pick him up on your way home."

"Call if you need me. You know, as a deputy."

Okay, she had to fight hard against the urge to laugh at the note of panic in his voice. She didn't want to risk hurting his feelings. "Conner, it was a simple kiss." That was a lie. There was nothing simple about it at all, but she knew he needed to clear his head before returning to work. "Don't let it cross your mind."

He didn't respond. Instead, he picked up his hat

off the table and started toward the front door. But along the way, he mumbled something under his breath that sounded something like "Fat chance of that," but she couldn't be sure.

He stopped by the pair on the floor in front of the television. "I have to go back to work now, Mia. Would you mind if Mutt hung out with you for a while? It might only be until I get home from work later tonight, or maybe he'll stay until sometime tomorrow morning."

She gave him a happy smile but then immediately frowned as she pointed toward her open mouth. "You're asking if there's something for him to eat while he's here. Good question. If it ends up that he's going to stay overnight, I'll put his breakfast in a plastic container and leave it on your front porch. Is that okay?"

Evidently Mia figured she'd done her due diligence when it came to taking care of Mutt. She turned her attention back to her show after offering Conner a cursory wave of her hand. Jody had a question of her own. "I'll put a bowl of water out for him after you leave. Do you let him up on the furniture?"

"Yeah, but I'll leave that up to you. He'd probably appreciate a blanket on the floor next to Mia's bed, but he's not picky."

By that point, she and Conner were both standing out on her porch. "I'll text you if I need you to come get Mutt, but I'm betting he'll be fine spending the night with Mia."

"Like I said, I'll leave food on your porch after I get home."

He started for his car, but turned back. "Lock up after you go in. If Mutt wants out, let him loose in your backyard. He won't go anywhere, and it won't hurt to let his presence be known if someone is watching."

She shivered at the thought of someone lurking out there in the darkness. "We'll be careful. Promise you'll do the same."

"I will. Now go on and head back inside."

She did as he ordered, but she watched from the front window until he backed out of the driveway and drove off into the darkness.

Three days later Conner found himself back in Detective Galloway's office. It had taken him that long to catch up with the man. He'd filled the detective in on the events of the other night. Well, not everything. He didn't need to know about the kiss.

"So you believe her. You know, about locking the door before she left for the day."

Conner gritted his teeth to keep from snarling at the detective. If their roles were reversed, he would've asked the same question. "She has no reason to lie and every reason to want to keep Mia safe."

Galloway leaned back in his chair, the springs protesting loudly. "It's still not enough for me to ask for police protection for them. The brass would laugh me out of the room if I even bothered to try."

"I know."

Budgets were always tight, and Conner hadn't been able to provide any hard proof that someone had broken into Jody's place. "I wanted to make sure to keep you in the loop."

When he started to stand up, Galloway motioned him to sit back down. "I'm glad you did, mainly because I was going to call you today."

The detective sat back up and brought up a file on his laptop. From the way he was clenching his teeth, the news wasn't going to be good. "We've started getting reports back on the body and car we found down in that ravine. The victim's fingerprints match the ones on Mia's backpack, but they still aren't in the system. We're still waiting on the DNA results, but they've promised to have it for us within the week. The lab is always backed up on stuff like that, but I managed to convince the brass that the case is likely connected to Mia. They've ordered everything be given priority."

So it was a good-news, bad-news scenario. "The bottom line is some progress has been made, but currently we're not much farther along than we were."

For the first time, the detective smiled. "Well, that would be true except for one thing. There were prints on the booster seat. Most were from the man, but the rest match Mia's."

Conner took a second to process that bombshell. "So she was in that car at some point, even if we don't know why."

"Pretty much, but it's a start. I'm hoping there'll be more to come that will help answer that question." He picked up a pen and tapped it on his desk, more of a nervous habit than a hint for Conner to leave. "I'm guessing you're keeping an eye on the area behind your houses."

There was no use in denying it. "When I can, and I take Mutt with me."

"Has he picked up anything new?"

"Not since the night when Jody found the door open. That's when he followed pretty much the same trail as the last break-in attempt. Straight from her patio to the back fence."

Galloway dropped the pen. "Keep me informed about anything new. I'll do the same."

Taking the comment as a dismissal, Conner got up to leave. But as he reached the door, Galloway spoke again. "I heard you were seen at the diner with a pretty woman and a little girl."

Conner should've known better than to take them there. "We ran into each other at church and decided to go out for pancakes afterward."

Galloway held up his hand as if to stave off the excuses. "I'm not judging you, Deputy. I'm well aware that this situation isn't normal for any of us. But emotional entanglements can muddy the waters, and I need you to keep your head in the game. Ms. Kruse needs that, too."

He puffed up his cheeks and then let out a slow breath. "I have a bad feeling that things are about

to heat up fast. My gut says the person who shot
that guy has been checking back regularly to see if
the body has been discovered. If that's the case, it's
a pretty safe bet they know by now. Who knows,
maybe the man was the real target, and the suspect
is only worried that we'll figure out who pulled the
trigger."

The detective didn't sound like he believed that.
Neither did Conner. "That wouldn't explain why
someone has been circling around Jody and Mia."

"Exactly. Like I said, keep your head in the game."

As Conner headed out on patrol, he pondered the
situation. They still had no idea who was behind
the murder or what the reason for the attack might
have been. Until they verified the identity of the man
who'd had Mia in his car, they couldn't begin to
guess what the shooter's endgame was. The culprit
might be content to sit back and hope the trail went
cold. On the other hand, the knowledge the police
now had about the car and the body might spur the
culprit into desperate action.

As he drove through the county, he couldn't quit
thinking about Galloway's warning to keep his head
in the game. The man was right. To do anything less
would only endanger the two people who had come
to mean so much to Conner in such a short time. No
one would fault him for becoming attached to Mia
with her huge eyes and stubborn chin. Watching her
and Mutt together was nothing short of adorable.

But Jody was a whole different matter. He'd clearly

been fooling himself that it was only Mia he was really worried about. A case could be made that he'd only offered a bit of human kindness when he'd held Jody close when she was scared. Never mind how right it had felt that she'd turned to him for comfort.

He didn't know about her, but he was still feeling the effect of that kiss. Whatever had possessed him to do such a thing? The truth was that he'd been wanting to kiss her since he'd cooked dinner for them the night she'd been run off the road. Even thinking about how close he'd come to losing her had kept him up pacing the floor for hours.

Since he couldn't be there to watch over them in the evenings, he'd assigned his surrogate that duty. Mutt now took Conner getting ready for work as a signal that it was time for him to head next door. Conner had made it clear to Jody that it was up to her if she wanted a watchdog every night. It spoke to how worried she was that she didn't hesitate. Mia, of course, was thrilled to have Mutt hanging out with her every night that Conner wasn't home.

He checked the time. His sergeant had asked him to join in on a speed trap starting around seven o'clock. The local residents had filed a complaint about the number of people speeding along a particular stretch of two-lane highway every evening. Maybe it would keep him busy enough to help make the rest of his shift pass quickly.

Luck was with him. He was about to turn onto

the highway when a car roared past him. It might be wrong to be happy that someone was about to get hit with a sizable fine. However, Conner had responded to too many accidents caused by people driving like the rules didn't apply to them. He flipped on his lights and hit the gas.

"Come on, Mutt."

Conner gave the leash a hard tug, reminding the dog which of them was supposed to be in charge. The downside of Mutt spending so much time at Jody's was that he thought that's where he was headed any-time they left home. "We both need some exercise. Besides, it's my day off, so you'll stay home with me."

That wouldn't make either Mutt or Mia happy, but Conner had plans for himself and the dog this morn-ing. He hadn't said anything to Jody, but he really missed having Mutt with him when he walked after getting home from work. So today they would go for a run and exercise some muscles neither of them had been using nearly enough. Afterward, they'd do a cool-down lap as they explored the greenbelt behind the houses. Jody hadn't reported any more problems, but that didn't mean trouble wasn't still lurking close by.

"Let's kick it up a notch, dog."

Mutt dutifully picked up speed, following the route they usually took through the neighborhood. Before turning back toward home, Conner circled

the park where the climber was. They'd almost completed a full circuit around the place when Mutt came
to an abrupt halt. He planted his nose in the grass
and began tracking something…or maybe someone.
The only time he'd acted this way in recent memory was the two times he'd picked up a scent trail in
Jody's backyard.

Conner let him sniff his fill. "Dog, this isn't the
first time I've wished you could talk. I'd love to know
if you've found some trace of the person who's been
on Jody's patio or if suddenly you find the scent of
squirrels impossible to ignore. So, which is it?"

After following the trail to the edge of the parking lot, Mutt ended his hunt as abruptly as it had
begun. That answered Conner's question. Squirrels
and other critters didn't suddenly go airborne in a
parking lot, thereby ending their scent trail. People,
on the other hand, got into vehicles and drove off.
Dogs like Mutt were good, but there was nothing
they could do when a trail went dead.

Time to check out the greenbelt. Conner went to
the opposite end from where they usually entered the
woods. He kept them at a slow but deliberate pace as
they zigzagged between the trees. Mutt was enjoying
himself, pausing occasionally to circle a particular
bush or tree with his nose to the ground to check out
what other dogs had stopped there recently. After
leaving his own marker, he continued on.

That behavior continued until they reached the
stretch of woods directly behind the houses on

their street. Mutt had been doing a routine sweep around the base of a large pine tree when he froze and backed up. Whining a little as if frustrated, he took another pass through the immediate area. Apparently more sure of what he'd found, Mutt lunged forward in pursuit of something or someone, almost yanking Conner off his feet in the process.

He considered letting Mutt off his leash to hunt on his own but decided against it. He might treat Mutt as if he were still working K-9 patrol, but he was pretty sure the authorities wouldn't agree that was a good idea. Still, he praised the dog. "That's it, Mutt. Show me."

Then he added the German word that meant "search" to Mutt. "*Voran*, boy."

He laughed when Mutt gave him a disgruntled look, as if he were saying, "What do you think I've been doing, boss?"

By that point they were behind the house on the other side of Jody's. Mutt slowed down, finally coming to a complete halt next to a cluster of waist-high bushes. Conner squatted down to take a better look at what had caught Mutt's attention.

There was a cigarette butt tucked back under the lowest branches of the bush. He gently pushed the branches aside and spotted several more, all the same brand of filtered cigarettes. Circling around to the other side of the bushes, he found more litter scattered on the ground. It looked as if someone had been spending a lot of time in that spot.

The question was whether they'd stood watch long enough to smoke that many cigarettes in one outing or whether they'd been there on several different occasions. Could be either one.

He did a slow turn, looking in all directions. There wasn't much to be seen from that spot to either side or the direction away from the houses. From where he stood, it was also hard to see over the cedar fencing that ran along the back edge of the property lines. So why this particular vantage point? On impulse, he pushed his way into the center of the bushes and found the answer. There was a large flat boulder in the center. Once he stepped up on top of it, he had an unobstructed view of Jody's back door. Rather than picking up any of the litter himself, he snapped a couple of pictures and texted them to Galloway's number before giving the detective a call. "If you're available, I have something I think you should take a look at. I won't touch anything until you get here, but we might want to see if your buddies in the lab have time to run a few more tests."

"I can be there inside fifteen minutes."

That was faster than Conner had expected. He stared across the distance toward Jody's house. "I'll meet you at the far end of the greenbelt and lead you in. I'd rather Jody not know about this until you see it."

After giving Galloway directions, Conner led Mutt back down the way they'd come. Like the detective had said back in his office, things were starting to heat up. With every step he took, Conner asked for God's help in protecting Jody and Mia. At the same time, he strengthened his own resolve to stand between the potential fire coming for his neighbor and the little girl.

FOURTEEN

Something was off about Conner's behavior, but Jody couldn't put her finger on what was bothering her. He'd continued the pattern of dropping Mutt off as he left for work and picking him up in the morning. He was just as warm and friendly with Mia as he'd been almost from the beginning. On the other hand, they hadn't shared any more impromptu meals, and he hadn't been at church on Sunday. Mia had grudgingly shared her hymnal with Jody instead, but both had missed having Conner there beside them.

Maybe the problem was work related. He hadn't mentioned any progress on Mia's case, which was worrisome. Mr. Greve had called again the previous afternoon. He'd mentioned being in frequent contact with Detective Galloway. Surely if he'd learned anything, he would've kept the caseworker informed.

So, if it wasn't the case that had Conner on edge, it had to be the kiss.

It was hard to not be a little insulted by that realization. After all, he'd started it. And now she sounded like one of her third graders pointing at someone else's behavior to defend her own poor choices.

"Is something funny?"

Okay, this was awkward. She didn't really want to admit that she'd lost track of whatever it was that Conner had been telling her. If she explained why she was smiling, she'd also have to explain what had led her train of thought to that particular station. "Nothing. It was only a stray thought."

Now that she was back in the moment, she focused her attention on Conner and what he'd been telling her. "Run that last part by me again."

His frustration was clear, but he patiently went back to the beginning as he started talking. "I think you should pack up Mia and go somewhere else. Maybe stay with your foster parents for a few days."

While she wouldn't reject the idea out of hand, she also wasn't sure it was the best plan of action. "Why now?"

He ran his fingers through his hair, the thick blond waves already rumpled as if it wasn't the first time he'd done that. "Because it would be safer for both of you. It wouldn't be for long. Just until we get a few things figured out."

"I assume that 'we' means you and Detective Galloway."

"Yeah."

"Ordinarily, this wouldn't the best time for me to leave town."

She held up her hand to cut off whatever protest he was about to make. "At least hear me out. Summer is already winding down, which means I have to report back to work soon. Between then and now, I need to make daycare arrangements for Mia. Start making lesson plans. Buy new supplies for my classroom and all the other things teachers do to get ready for the new school year."

"Surely you can afford a few days away."

It was obvious this was important to him. "Yes, if it's absolutely necessary in order to keep Mia safe. But you have to understand that my real concern is that Mia is just now getting settled into a routine. I'm concerned about the effects uprooting her again might have."

As she spoke, a few puzzle pieces finally snapped together. "Conner, what has changed? You obviously think the two of us are in greater danger for some reason. What's happened that you haven't told me?"

"I'm not in charge of the case."

"That's not an answer." On second thought, maybe it was. "So Detective Galloway hasn't given you the okay to keep me informed about the situation even though the trouble is likely to land right on my doorstep."

Without giving him a chance to respond, she took out her cell phone and called the other man herself. "Detective, it's Jody Kruse here. Since it is apparent Deputy Dunne hasn't been authorized to inform me about what is going on, I suggest you tell me. Otherwise, my next calls will be to your supervisor to file a complaint. Why not make things simpler for everyone and simply come talk to me? I'll put on a pot of coffee and maybe even bake some cookies. Be here while they're still warm from the oven, or I'll be making that call."

Jody hung up before the sputtering detective could get a word in edgewise. She offered Conner a small smile when his phone rang five seconds later. Turning her back on him, she walked away. "I guess I should get started on those cookies."

Forty-five minutes later, a dark sedan pulled into Jody's driveway and a disgruntled-looking Detective Galloway got out. Rather than heading for her house, he walked around the hedge toward Conner's front door. Fine. Let the two of them confer on how best to deal with her. Surely they could understand why she needed to know what was going on. How could she make the best decision for Mia without knowing all the facts?

She arranged the cookies on a plate and set them in the middle of the table. The coffee was ready, and she'd made a pot of tea for herself. Everything was in place except for putting on a movie for Mia to watch while the adults talked.

She peeked in on Mia. "Deputy Dunne and his friend are on their way over to talk with me. While we do that, I thought you might enjoy watching a movie on the television in my bedroom. I'm sure Mutt is coming over to keep you company."

It didn't take the little girl long to choose her movie. "Take it to my room. I'll be right in to put it on for you. I'll also put together some snacks for you and Mutt."

Mia had just scampered off down the hall when the doorbell rang. Jody had been heading toward the kitchen but did an immediate detour to welcome the two men into her home. Well, sort of, anyway.

"Detective Galloway, thanks for coming. Deputy Dunne, Mia is waiting for Mutt in my room. They're going to watch a movie together while we talk. It won't take me long to get things organized for them."

She plated up a cookie and apple slices for Mia and added three of the organic dog treats she kept around for Mutt. Meanwhile, the two men made themselves at home in her kitchen, fixing their coffee before settling in at the table to wait for her to join them.

"Come on, Mutt. Mia is this way."

The dog pushed past her in search of his friend. After starting the movie, Jody left Mia and Mutt to enjoy themselves. Too bad she couldn't hang out with the two of them. It was sure to be a lot more fun than what she was facing in the other room.

She remained silent until she'd poured herself a cup of tea and carefully chosen the perfect cookie out of the pile. The entire time, she was aware of two pairs of male eyes tracking her every move. It was hard to be certain, but she kind of thought that they were both a little concerned about what she might do next.

Satisfied that she had their attention, she smiled first at the detective and then at Conner. "Okay, gentlemen. Start talking."

Conner sat back, his cop face on full display as he crossed his arms over his chest. Jody took that to mean two things. First, that he was there in his professional capacity, not as a friend. And second, he expected the detective to lead the discussion. Galloway took one more sip of his coffee and set the cup back down on the table.

Looking only marginally more relaxed than Conner, he launched right in. "For the record, Ms. Kruse, I called Dale Greve earlier this morning to catch him up on the case. You were on my list of people to call, as was Conner. Most of what I'm about to tell you has only come to light in the past two days."

She glanced at Conner, who barely nodded as if to quietly confirm what she was being told was the truth. "So, Detective, do I owe you and Deputy Dunne an apology for threatening to call your supervisor?"

He actually grinned at her. "Not necessary, Ms. Kruse. We're well aware that the circumstances in a case like this aren't easy for anybody."

"No, they aren't, but don't take that to mean that having Mia living with me is a problem. She's a real joy to have around. It's all of the other stuff that's been hard." Then she offered a small smile of her own. "And please, call me Jody. 'Ms. Kruse' is my teacher name, and you two definitely aren't third graders."

Judging by the deep lines life had carved around the detective's eyes and mouth, it had been a long, long time since he'd lost the innocence of childhood. Conner had some of that same edge at times, but it had yet to leave its mark on him. Well, at least on the outside. She suspected what he dealt with on a day-to-day basis would always have long-term effects on a person.

"First, I've received word Mrs. Caldwell has been transferred to an extended-care facility in Spokane. Sadly, she doesn't remember anything about the attack that's useful."

"That sounds like she's doing better. I've been praying for her."

"That was the good news, but I should warn you that some of this will be tough to hear. If it gets to be too much or if you need a break, let me know."

Just that quickly, Jody regretted eating a cookie. After pushing her plate aside, she folded her hands in her lap to hide the way they were now shaking. Threading her fingers together, she waited for him to share the bad news.

"Recently some hikers discovered a car that had gone off the road and rolled down a hillside into a ravine. Unfortunately, the driver didn't survive."

She offered up a silent prayer for the man and his

loved ones as the detective continued with his narrative. "We had to wait until the autopsy to know if he died from injuries from the accident or from the bullet wound in his chest."

Every drop of blood in her head drained away, leaving Jody light-headed and even more queasy. She was dimly aware that Conner was up and moving. A few seconds later, he held a cool, damp cloth to her forehead. "You'll be all right, Jody."

That was doubtful, but at least the room had quit spinning. Mostly, anyway. He stepped away to refresh the cloth under the faucet. "Thanks, Conner. I'm feeling better."

He studied her for several seconds as if trying to decide if that was true before returning to his seat. Galloway looked apologetic. "I know this is difficult, but you wanted to know everything that we've learned. I happen to think that's a good idea. So does Conner."

"This all comes as a bit of a shock. I'll be fine now." *Maybe.* "So who was he?"

"We're still working on that. His fingerprints aren't in the system, and the ID in his wallet was fake. He paid for the car with cash using the same false information, and the license plates were stolen. The man was definitely flying under the radar."

He looked up from his notes to see how she was doing. When she offered him a shaky smile, he continued on. "There were no skid marks on the road that might have indicated the involvement of another vehicle in the incident."

"So you don't know if he was run off the road or if he lost control."

The memory of her own experience with a similar situation sent chills through her. Not that she'd been shot. But if that farm track hadn't been right there when she needed it, the outcome would've been so much worse.

"To be honest, we suspect the reason he lost control was most likely a combination of someone running him off the road and the blood loss from being shot."

"If you know so little about him, why do you think this is somehow tied to Mia?"

"That's where it gets interesting. The car had a booster seat in the back, and we were able to recover fingerprints from it. One set is definitely Mia's."

Jody asked the next obvious question. "So was the driver her father?"

"We didn't know at first. It took time for the lab to run the DNA tests for comparison. The results just came back with a paternal match. I'm sorry to say the victim was definitely Mia's father."

Conner spoke up. "But there was no sign of her mother being in the car."

Galloway shook his head. "As far as we can tell, it was only the two of them. At this point, we also don't know what made him abandon Mia at the hospital."

He closed his notebook and finished off his coffee. "There are obviously a lot of unanswered questions. Where was he headed? Why not take Mia with him? Why is no one else looking for her? If the two of them suddenly disappeared and went into hiding for some reason, you'd think at least someone would be asking questions. If not Mia's mother, then some other members of the family. Even coworkers might wonder where they were."

His frustration was obvious, as was Conner's. She had one possible thing to share that might help the detective make sense of the situation. "When Mia first came, we asked about her mother. She shrugged and shook her head. She didn't seem upset or scared or anything like that. It was more like she either didn't have one or that she wasn't around for some reason."

If that was true, poor Mia had now lost her only remaining parent. What a nightmare.

Well, Mia had her, and she also had Conner, not to mention Mutt. With God's help, the three of them would help guide her through all this. She was sure the caseworkers and even Detective Galloway would be right there with them.

But back to the matter at hand. "So you think he was the target, not Mia?"

The detective had been reaching for another cookie, but he withdrew his hand. "Again, we don't know. My gut feeling is that he dropped Mia off where he hoped she'd be safe and then tried to lead whoever was after him away from the area. He didn't get all that far before his car careened off the road. As a crow flies, the ravine is less than fifteen miles from the hospital."

Jody might not be a cop herself, but she could see where he was going with this. "You think the shooter is still in the area and looking for Mia."

Conner spoke up, his eyes full of sympathy, as if he already knew how much of a blow his next words were going to be. "No, we think the shooter knows exactly where she is."

Jody had been so hoping that wasn't what he was going to say. "You both think that's who tried to break in and ran me off the road."

He nodded. "And maybe even was watching us that day at the park."

Hoping Detective Galloway felt differently about all that, she directed her next question to him. "And do you think that, too?"

"Regrettably, yes. Deputy Dunne recently found a spot out in the greenbelt within sight of your house. The evidence indicates someone may have been standing out there for some time. Unfortunately, we have no way of knowing when that was or if it was only on a single occasion or multiple times. We have the lab processing the evidence to see what they can learn."

By that point, Conner was practically vibrating with tension. Jody knew exactly how he felt. "So this is why you thought I should pack up Mia and take off to stay with the Burkses."

He nodded, but Detective Galloway didn't seem

to know what she was talking about. "I was placed in foster care myself when I was in my early teens. I lived with the Burkses until I got a job teaching on this side of the mountains four years ago."

Jody poured herself another cup of tea as she considered what she wanted to say next. Too restless to sit back down, she leaned against the counter and did her best to put her thoughts into good order. "They're good people who wouldn't hesitate to take us in. They've even met Mia, because we went over to visit them for a day. Having said that, I don't think that's a good idea for several reasons. For starters, Papa Burks has a heart condition and doesn't need the added stress. I would never lie to them about why we needed to move in, and he would worry."

The detective slowly nodded. "I can understand that."

She continued. "I suppose we could check in to a hotel somewhere, but we don't even know if you're looking for a man or a woman. All we know is the person who ran me off the road was driving a gray or silver SUV, which are a dime a dozen these days. If my house is being watched, it wouldn't be hard for them to figure out we were leaving and follow us to the hotel. All we do know for sure is that whoever is after Mia has already killed one man. I won't put anyone else at risk. Besides, I feel safer here knowing Mutt and Conner are right next door."

Then she stood up. "Thank you for coming, Detective Galloway. You've given me a lot to think about.

For now, I feel safer here where the police are keeping a close eye on the situation. Having said that, I'll pack a few things in case we need to leave in a hurry."

Detective Galloway offered her a small smile. "Good idea. I'll also do better about keeping you in the loop."

"I'd appreciate that. Now, I should check on Mia. Feel free to take the cookies with you. Conner knows where I keep the plastic bags."

As she headed for the bedroom, Jody turned back. "I really, really wish this was all over with."

Neither man spoke, but their expressions made it clear that they knew just how she felt.

FIFTEEN

"Boy, she's really something."

Conner couldn't argue with the detective's assessment of Jody, but that didn't mean he was happy about it. After leaving Jody's house, Detective Galloway had invited Conner to a nearby restaurant to discuss the situation further over burgers and fries. In between bites, Galloway said, "I've got to admire her determination to see this through, though. When it comes to Mia, that woman has a spine of pure steel."

Jody definitely had her moments. Conner suspected that she'd throw herself between Mia and anyone who threatened the little girl. But he also remembered how badly shaken Jody had been the day she'd been run off the road and when someone tried to break into the house.

Galloway washed the last of his burger down with a big gulp of iced tea. "She clearly thinks a lot of you, Deputy."

Conner hoped he wasn't blushing as he dipped a

fry in ketchup and ate it. "I've been leaving Mutt with her when I'm at work, but I can't be next door 24-7 to keep an eye on things. And unless we put Jody in a complete lockdown, whoever is out there can get to her whenever she leaves the house."

The thought made him sick. He could be on patrol handing out speeding tickets while a killer had Jody and Mia in his sights.

"Get her to agree to a few restrictions for the short term. You know, like maybe having her groceries delivered. If Jody does have to run an errand, have her set it up for a time when you can go with them. She can also call me if all else fails."

The detective held up his hand to stop Conner from interrupting. "I think it's smart of you to leave your dog with her while you're at work. Even if the suspect is watching the house from the greenbelt, it would take a braver person than I am to take on Mutt."

That much was true. "Okay, I'll talk to her."

They concentrated on their meal for the next few minutes. Galloway needed to get back to the office, and Conner wanted to talk to Jody again before he had to leave for work. As they finished up, the detective threw his credit card down on the table, waving off Conner's attempt to pay for his own meal.

"Lunch is the least I can do considering how much extra time you've been putting in on this case."

Conner snarled a little. "It's my job, Detective. Just like it's yours."

The man looked more amused than offended by the show of temper. "All things considered, I think you can drop the 'Detective' and call me Jack. And I know it's your job, Conner, but this one is more than that for you. You care about both Jody and Mia. You don't have to admit it to me, but at least be honest with yourself about it."

"Emotions only complicate things."

Their server returned with Jack's credit card, so he stopped to sign the check before responding. When she walked away, he met Conner's gaze head-on. "Yeah, they do. And as nice as it would be to be able to shut down our feelings while on the job, that's not possible. You'll be better off in the long run if you learn to deal with them. Some cases are bound to get to you more than others. This is one of those for both of us. I'm worried we'll miss something and either Mia or Jody will pay the price. I'm also frustrated that we can't figure out why no one is looking for that little girl. I don't want Mia to end up in the system while someone who loves her ends up never knowing what happened to her."

He threw some cash on the table for a tip and started for the door, leaving Conner to follow in his wake. When they got outside, Jack spun back around and got all up in Conner's personal space. "Personally, I take all of my frustrations out on a punching bag when everything gets to be too much. It helps clear my head. If you have the same problem, find some way to work through the stress so it doesn't clog your thinking."

"I go running."

"If that works for you, good. It will help keep the job from eating you alive." Then Galloway poked a finger toward Conner's chest. "I figure there's something more to what you're feeling for Jody. You can tell me to kiss off, and I wouldn't blame you. But don't miss out on the chance for something special with her because of the job. In my experience, the best cops find some way to balance the job and whatever else life has to offer."

Then he simply walked away.

Conner considered taking the scenic route back home. That would be both stupid and cowardly, and he'd prefer not to think of himself in those terms. Jody was depending on him to help keep her and Mia safe. He should be there at least until he had to leave for work.

The thought of his chosen profession sent his emotions into another tailspin. Everything Detective Galloway—Jack—had said to him had hit home hard. Yes, he cared about Jody and Mia far more than he should under the circumstances.

Jack was also right about there being more to life than the job, but somehow Conner had forgotten that. Looking back, he could remember what it was like to be part of a family and how special it had been. He'd been the center of his parents' world, and they'd been his anchors. They'd taught him about faith and the role it should play in his life. Losing them had shaken the foundations of everything he'd depended on.

Yes, Grandpa Jasper had offered him a safe haven, something for which he would always be grateful. Even so, life with his grandfather had been very different, so much more solitary.

Avoiding emotional entanglements with other people was Jasper's way of protecting himself from the pain of losing them. Conner understood why his grandfather felt that way—he'd lost his wife after a long illness and soon after his only son and daughter-in-law to a drunk driver. The pain had to have been crippling. Maybe keeping his heart safe was the only way Jasper could hold it together long enough to raise Conner.

So they'd fished together, hunted together, camped together. It somehow got to be a habit of spending time with only each other for company. While comfortable and safe, it was also lonely, especially after Jasper died. He'd been ready to go, wanting to be reunited with his loving wife and son. Conner understood that even though it had meant that he was suddenly alone in the world.

He took a hard look at himself in the rearview mirror and shook his head. He couldn't help but think that was a metaphor for his life. Always looking back and wondering what might have been if that drunk driver had decided to call a cab instead of driving himself home. Maybe it was time to look forward, to see if he could find a better way of doing things, of finding that balance that Jack had been rattling on about.

Even taking responsibility for Mutt had been a major change in Conner's life. After Jasper's death, Conner hadn't had to worry about the welfare of anyone else outside the confines of his job. Having someone waiting for him to get home from work, even if that someone was furry, had felt strange at first. Now he couldn't imagine walking into his house after work and not seeing Mutt sprawled on the couch waiting for him.

Not that he'd been there the past few nights. He'd been next door with Jody and Mia, watching over them when Conner couldn't be there to do it himself. He missed his dog, but he wasn't selfish enough to reclaim Mutt in the middle of the night if having him at her place helped Jody and Mia sleep better.

To be honest, he was also jealous of Mutt. Somehow opening his home and his heart to a dog who needed him had also opened Conner's heart up to caring about Jody and Mia. He already knew that Jody cared about him, too. When she told him to stay safe when he left for work, those weren't merely hollow words. There was caring and worry laced through every syllable.

But before they could figure out what was happening between the two of them, they had to end the threat to Mia. Whatever it took, they had to make sure she stayed safe. Until she was, none of them could move forward.

As he finally turned on to their street, he smiled. Just a little, anyway. After all, the threat that hung over their heads wouldn't last forever. Then maybe he would kiss Jody again and see where that led them.

The meeting with Detective Galloway and Conner had gone better than Jody had expected. Her heart ached for Mia. Eventually, someone would have to explain to the little girl what had happened to her father. Most likely that would fall to Jody as Mia's foster parent, or to her caseworker. It would be a tough discussion, but it would be better for Mia to learn the truth from people who cared about her and whom she already trusted.

One question had started rolling around in Jody's head ever since the detective had shared the DNA findings and what they meant for Mia's future. What if they never located any family? Or if they did, what if that person either wouldn't or couldn't take care of Mia? What would happen to her then?

Jody knew firsthand that a stable foster home like the Burkses' could make all the difference in a kid's life. But the threat of bureaucrats' sometimes capricious decisions and government budget cuts had always hovered in the background. Kids could get moved with no warning and no explanation. Regardless, Jody would fight to keep Mia with her. The little girl already owned a big piece of Jody's heart, and it hurt to think about how lonely her life would be with Mia no longer in it.

And what if Mia were to become eligible for adoption? If that happened, Jody would also fight to be at the front of the line. Her chief worry was that the courts might prefer to place Mia with a couple, but Jody hoped she'd be given serious consideration since Mia already knew her. She would also ask Mrs. Caldwell and Pastor Dahl for their personal recommendations. But that was a worry for another day.

A familiar car pulled in next door. Conner was back home and headed straight for her door. He hadn't been all that happy about her wanting to talk to the detective in person, so she'd figured he'd probably already had enough of her company for one day.

Maybe he wanted to spend time with Mutt before he had to leave for work, which was something else she felt a little guilty about. Yes, she was worried about whoever had been lurking around her house, but commandeering Conner's dog for the duration wasn't exactly fair to him...or even the dog, she supposed.

Any efforts they'd talked about to prevent Mia from getting too attached to both Mutt and Conner had long gone by the wayside. Once things returned to normal, it was going to be hard to explain to Mia why Mutt had to go back to living next door instead of sleeping on the foot of the little girl's bed at night. Jody wasn't sure she approved of dogs on the furniture, but even she didn't have the heart to put a stop to it now.

She waited until Conner knocked to open the door. "Come in."

He seemed hesitant but crossed the threshold. "I wanted to see how you were doing. Jack dumped a whole lot of heavy stuff on you while he was here."

"Yeah, he did, but I'm grateful that the two of you told me everything that's going on."

"It was still scary."

"It was, but I appreciated his honesty."

Conner studied her for a few seconds before lifting his hand to rest against her cheek. He kept the touch light, but it soothed her jangled nerves. "I can't tell you how sorry I am about both you and Mia having to deal with all of this. I know you shield her from it as much as possible, but she still must wonder why her dad hasn't come for her."

His hand dropped away, and he took a step back. "It's also easy to understand why she was so traumatized by whatever led up to him leaving her sitting at the hospital."

That same thrum of tension she'd sensed in Conner earlier when they first sat down for their little talk with the detective was back again. There was something else he wanted to say, but he didn't know where to start. She gave him a prod. "I can tell you have more you need to tell me, but you're obviously worried it will upset me. I can't promise it won't, but I will promise to listen. Me trying to guess whatever has you all tied up in knots only makes it harder for both of us. Just tell me."

He flexed his hands several times as if trying to find some way to relax before he finally spoke. When he did, the words poured out in a rush. "Fine. You made some good points about why you and Mia going to ground in a hotel wouldn't work. Having said that, we also don't think it's a good idea for you to leave the house more than absolutely necessary. One suggestion Jack made was for you to have your groceries delivered."

Huh. The idea had never occurred to her. "I've never done that."

Conner looked even more frustrated. "Okay, if that doesn't work for you, then at least run your errands when I'm around so I can go with you."

Clearly patience was in short supply today, but she reined in her own temper. "I didn't say I wouldn't do it, Conner, only that I've never done it. I'll give it a try. It's not like I have to do it forever."

He looked marginally happier. "Do you have any errands that can't be handled from home?"

She checked the calendar on her phone. "Nothing I can't postpone, except that Mia is scheduled to see the counselor again on Wednesday morning. We have to be there at eleven."

"Okay, I can take you and bring you back."

She couldn't resist asking a semisnarky question. "Isn't providing chauffeur service sort of going above and beyond what your job requires?"

His smile was a bit rueful. "It would be if keeping the two of you safe was only part of my job description. It's not and hasn't been for a long time."

The man was sure confusing. "But you've said—"

He shook his head. "I know what I said, Jody, but I was lying. Mostly to myself, but to you, too. I'm done with that."

She was saved from having to reply because Mutt came charging into the room with Mia hot on his heels. The dog pranced around Conner before stopping right in front of him, his front legs down flat on the ground, his backside in the air, and his tail wagging as if daring his buddy to play. Jody backed out of reach, taking Mia with her to give the pair room to maneuver.

But instead of taking to the floor with Mutt, Conner headed straight for the door to the backyard. "Come on, Mutt. We can't trash Jody's living room."

The dog followed right behind him, squeezing past Conner to be the first out the door. Jody took Mia's hand. "Come on, let's go watch the silliness."

They took front-row seats on the patio while man and dog chased each other around the yard. Mutt barked and dodged forward and then danced backward out of reach. Then in a surprise move, he charged right back and put his front paws on Conner's shoulders. He laughed and let the dog's weight take them both to the ground, man and dog having a great time growling as each one tried to claim victory.

Finally, Conner stopped moving long enough to say, "Enough, boy."

They both stayed on the ground while they caught their breath. Mia clapped to express her appreciation for their antics. Mutt loped back over to the patio to quench his thirst from the water bowl that Mia kept filled to the brim for him. Jody ducked back into the kitchen long enough to grab a bottle of water for Conner and tossed it to him as he pulled up another of the lawn chairs and sat down.

"Whew. I don't know about Mutt, but I needed that."

The dog flopped down on the cement and laid his head on Conner's foot with a contented sigh. Conner reached down to pat him on the head. "I miss you, too, big guy."

Jody winced. "I feel bad about hogging so much of Mutt's time."

"Don't." Conner gave her a considering look. "Seriously, if you're sleeping better with him here, then I can sleep better next door. It's only temporary."

Then he looked at Mia, who was now wandering around the edge of the yard. She stopped to sniff a bright red blossom before moving on. Every so often, she picked a flower to add to the small bouquet she was creating. When she approached a cluster of roses in the back corner, Jody called out, "Remember those have thorns, Mia."

She waited to make sure Mia understood before

turning back to Conner. "I know it's temporary, and I really appreciate that you let us borrow him. I'd forgotten how nice it was to have a dog around. My birth parents wouldn't let me have any pets, which was probably for the best. They had a hard enough time remembering to take care of me."

Conner reached over to give her hand a gentle squeeze. "I'm sorry they didn't appreciate what they had. Some people were never cut out to be parents. You have every right to be angry with them."

"Sorry, I didn't mean to bum you out. Don't forget that I was lucky and got a second chance at being part of a family with the Burkses. I let all of the anger go a long time ago. Most of it, anyway. I didn't do it all on my own, though. Obviously, the Burkses were a big part of my healing process. So were the counselors at school and the youth pastor at the church we attended."

"Do you have any kind of contact with your birth parents?"

"I saw them a couple of times early on. It wasn't pretty. Looking back, I think they might have felt guilty, and I was still so angry. Those emotions don't make for warm and fuzzy moments."

Conner was looking pretty grim by that point. "And none of your extended family expressed any interest in offering you a home?"

"There really wasn't anyone. My parents were both only children, and I didn't have any grandparents left.

I did meet my paternal grandmother a few times when I was little, but I only have vague memories of her. I was really surprised to learn she'd left me a trust fund that helped pay for college and the down payment on this house. I've always thought at least she must have cared for me to do something so generous."

She couldn't stand to learn if Conner was looking at her with pity, so she kept her eyes focused on Mia's journey around the yard. "I've often wondered if things would've been different if my folks hadn't inherited a lot of money from their parents' estates so early in their marriage."

Time to move on. "Again, I didn't mean to go all gloom and doom. A lot of people had a worse time of it."

"And you made the most of the opportunity that was given you. I'm betting the Burkses would tell you that you gave as much to their family as you got from them."

He finally released his hold on her hand to check the time on his watch. "I've got to get a move on and get ready for work."

After giving Mutt a thorough scratching, he stood up. "I'll pick up Mutt for a long run in the morning. Otherwise, I'm available for chauffeuring duties if something comes up."

"I hate tying up some much of your time, but I really appreciate it."

Mia had finally circled back to the patio. She

frowned as if wondering what was going on. "Conner has to leave to get ready for work, Mia."

The little girl immediately latched on to Mutt's collar. It wasn't clear if she was making her claim on the dog or only reminding Mutt that he was supposed to stay with them. The maneuver had the adults exchanging glances. Conner knew the arrangement was temporary. So did Jody. But they both knew when the time came, it was going to be really difficult to explain to Mia why Mutt would be moving back home next door full-time.

She wasn't the only one who might have a hard time when things went back to normal. Like if Conner went back to being just her next-door neighbor.

Then he did something to remind her that wasn't going to happen quite yet. Before leaving, he stood up on the lawn chair and stared out toward the trees, taking his time as he slowly scanned the greenbelt from the far right all the way to the left and back again. When he stepped back down, he'd definitely shifted into cop mode.

"See anything?"

"No."

That was a relief, but it didn't stop her from bringing Mia and Mutt back inside and securing all the doors as soon as Conner left. And later checking the locks two more times before going to bed. Even then, she struggled to relax enough to sleep. Then her eyes lit on a small plaque on her bedroom wall. It had been a housewarming gift from Mama Burks, something that had come down through her family and contained the Lord's Prayer written in faded gold script.

Smiling in the darkness, Jody whispered the prayer from memory. As she repeated it a second time, her tension started fading away.

Before she could finish it a third time, she was asleep.

SIXTEEN

It felt almost magical to have her groceries simply appear on the front porch. Now that Jody had tried it, she suspected she might take advantage of the service at times during the school year when there never seemed to be enough hours in the day. But that was a concern for another time. Right now, she needed to put away the last few items and then get Mia ready to go. Conner was driving them to see Dr. Mayberry in a few minutes.

If all went well, he wanted to take them out to lunch afterward. She didn't know about Mia, but Jody was really looking forward to that. Simply knowing that she had to stick so close to home right now left her feeling pretty claustrophobic. It didn't help that she also didn't feel comfortable spending much time out in the backyard. What if there was someone out there watching their every move? Worse yet, what if this time that person decided to attack?

All that had her checking the lock on the back

door and glancing out to make sure no one was in the yard. Feeling marginally better, she shoved her fears aside for the moment. She checked the time and called out, "Mia, come get your shoes on. We need to be ready to go before Conner comes over."

When there was no response, she tried again. "Come on, little one. Time to get a move on."

Finally, Jody gave up and went looking for the little girl. She found her sitting in the rocking chair in her room looking at books. It was nice that she enjoyed them, but now wasn't the time.

Jody had brought Mia's shoes with her, so she slipped them on while Mia continued to ignore her. After tying the shoelaces, Jody offered her a hand up off the rocker. "I know you're enjoying your books, but we have to go. You can bring one in the car with you, but we shouldn't keep Conner and Dr. Mayberry waiting."

No dice. Mia's face was locked into crabby-frown mode as she refused to acknowledge Jody's presence. It might've been funny if they weren't running short on time. Frustrated, Jody demanded, "Come on, Mia. Tell me what's wrong."

Okay, that wasn't going to get them anywhere. It wasn't as if the little girl would actually answer. But then she did in her own clever way. She held up the book about the German shepherd and pointed at the cover. Conner had come over earlier to reclaim his dog to take him on a long run. Mia hadn't liked waking up to find her friend had deserted her.

Jody understood why she felt that way, but it didn't change the fact that the dog belonged to Conner, not Mia and Jody. "I've explained before why Mutt needs to spend time with Conner, too. Dogs like Mutt need a lot of exercise, the kind neither of us can give him. I'm sure he'll be back over to visit later after we get home from seeing Dr. Mayberry."

Then she picked Mia up, leaving the little girl no choice but to come. They were running out of time, and she didn't want to be late for the counseling appointment. They made it all the way to the living room before Mia struggled to get down. Jody set her free but made sure to stay between the little rascal and the escape route back to her room.

"Did I mention that Conner said we could go out for lunch after your appointment if we do a good job today?"

Mia gave her a puzzled look, which Jody understood. What would doing a good job of going to an appointment even look like? "We need to be on time and not keep other people waiting. That includes both Conner and Dr. Mayberry. It would also be nice to get out of the house for a little while. Wouldn't you like to go to lunch with Conner?"

After giving it some thought, Mia nodded. Then she mimed climbing and made a swooping motion with her hand. Jody studied her for a few seconds. "You want to go to the park and play on the climber?"

That earned her an emphatic nod. "That would be fun, but we'll have to see what Conner says about it.

He's already using a lot of his free time to take us to the appointment and then lunch, but it won't hurt to ask him. If we can't go today, maybe we can go tomorrow. Now, let's hit the road."

Before opening the front door, she stopped long enough to text Conner that they were ready to go. He responded within seconds that he'd be right out after he called Mutt back in from the backyard. Before letting Mia join her out on the porch, Jody looked up and down the street. The coast appeared to be clear. She motioned for Mia to come outside and then locked the front door. The two of them started toward the driveway. Earlier, she had suggested to Conner that they should take her sedan to avoid the hassle of having to transfer Mia's booster seat to his SUV.

But as they approached the car, something about it looked strange. Why was it listing to one side like that? "Wait here a second, Mia."

Jody continued forward cautiously, being careful to make sure Mia stayed behind her. As soon as she rounded the car to the driver's side, the problem was obvious. Both tires on that side were flat, no doubt thanks to the long slashes that had been carved into the sidewalls. Her pulse jumped into high gear. It was imperative that they get back inside the house.

However, Mia was no longer standing where she'd left her. Jody spun in place, looking for her. The little girl had circled around the other side of the car and was heading straight for Conner's house. Struggling to remain calm, Jody tried to call her back. "Mia, come back. I've forgotten something, and we need to go back inside. Hurry."

When that didn't convince Mia, Jody started after her. If all else failed, she would snatch her up and run for Conner's front door. Her attention remained laser focused on the little girl. She'd just caught up with her and taken her hand when the sound of an approaching car had Jody spinning around to face the street.

A dark gray SUV screeched to a stop a few feet from where she stood. A second later, a strange woman climbed out of the driver's side but left the engine running. She was well-dressed and looked to be somewhere in her forties, maybe early fifties. After a brief glance at Mia, she turned back toward Jody. "You must be Jody Kruse."

"Yes."

"It's so nice to finally meet you. I understand that you've been taking care of Amelia." She offered Jody a too-bright smile, one that was surprisingly unnerving. "I'm here to pick up my daughter now that I've set up our new home."

So that was Mia's real name. It was amazing how close it was to the one that had been randomly chosen for her. She was going to say something to Mia, but she stopped as soon as she glanced down at her. The little girl's face had gone white, and she shook her head from side to side as she tried to back farther up Conner's driveway.

Jody tightened her grip on Mia's hand but turned

slightly to put herself directly between her and the woman. It was time to ask some questions. "And you would be?"

"Jennifer Stewart."

As she spoke, the woman shifted to the right to be able to look at Mia directly and held out her hand. "Come along, Amelia. It's time to go home. You've been very naughty staying away all this time. Your father tried to hide you from me, but Philip shouldn't have done that. He knew we belonged together. I told him we were a family, but he wouldn't listen."

Jody interrupted Jennifer's attempts to coax the little girl away from her. "How did you find us?"

The woman shot her a frustrated glance. "Obviously, the police told me where she was."

Nothing about that statement rang true. Jody injected a little more determination into her next question. "What's the name of the officer who told you to come here?"

Jennifer's eyes narrowed as she gave Jody a dismissive look. "I don't remember, but what does that matter? She's mine, and I'm taking her home."

It mattered because Jody knew full well neither Detective Galloway nor Dale Greve would've sent anyone to pick up Mia without contacting her first. That's not how these things were done. "I'm sorry, but I really must confirm what you're telling me. After all, we both want Mia to be safe. I'm sure you understand."

"No, in fact I don't." Jennifer moved another two

steps forward. "You're wasting my time, probably hoping to figure out some way to keep her here in order to get more money out of the state for her care. Sorry, but you'll have to figure out some other way to make a living."

Once again plastering a brittle smile on her face, she prattled on. "Amelia and I have a long drive ahead of us, and we should get started. And you should know that people who get between me and Amelia end up regretting it."

Jody really, really hoped that Conner was on his way out. The woman's barely veiled threat sent a surge of cold fear burning through Jody, not only for her own safety, but for Mia's as well. She slowly backed up another step and then another, making sure Mia kept pace with her.

"Let's discuss this calmly, Jennifer. Even if you're her mother, I need to call Mia's caseworker. I don't have the authority to release her to anyone else's custody. There are procedures that have to be followed."

By that point, Mia was fighting hard to get away from Jody, no doubt hoping to make a break for Conner's door. Jody took her eye off the woman long enough to comfort the terrified girl. "Don't worry, Mia, we'll figure this out. Conner will help us."

By the time she looked back, a gun had somehow appeared in Jennifer's hand. With no warning, she charged forward and swung the weapon at Jody's face. Jody managed to block the blow with her forearm, but the impact knocked her off balance. After hitting the ground hard, she struggled to get back up on her feet.

In the meantime, the woman had grabbed Mia by the arm. The little girl fought surprisingly hard to break free. Even so, Jennifer succeeded in dragging her several steps back toward her SUV, but she froze for an instant when a deep voice bellowed, "Police! Drop the gun and release the girl!"

Jennifer shrieked right back at Conner. "No! I'm taking her home! This farce has gone on long enough. She's mine, and you have no right to stop me."

Conner reached Jody just as she had staggered back up to her feet. He steadied her with one hand and held his gun in the other. He kept it aimed at the other woman as he asked, "Jody, are you all right?"

"Yeah, I'm fine." That was a total lie, but her own well-being wasn't important right now. She pleaded with the other woman. "Jennifer, you're scaring Amelia. Please, give us a chance to call the case-worker. I'm sure it's only a matter of everyone signing off on the right paperwork."

They all knew that wasn't true, so Jody's suggestion did nothing to de-escalate the situation. Conner remained stationary, never looking away from their adversary. In a low voice, he whispered, "I called it in. Help is on the way."

She nodded to acknowledge that she'd heard him. What a relief. Now they had to keep Jennifer talking long enough to stall until reinforcements arrived. Not knowing what else to do, Jody performed introductions. "Deputy Conner Dunne, this is Jennifer Stewart. She claims she's Mia's mother."

The woman sneered. "I am her mother, and her name isn't Mia. It's Amelia Douglas. She belongs with me, not you. I've been watching you for days, waiting for a chance to take her home without all of this fuss. You've forced my hand, though."

Jennifer kept her weapon aimed at Jody as she backed away. But when she finally dragged Mia within reach of the SUV, Jennifer had to either put down the gun or let go of Mia in order to open the door. As she hesitated, the gutsy little girl sank her teeth into her captor's left wrist. The woman yelped and instinctively released her hold on Mia in response to the pain. Before she could grab her again, Mia was off and running right to Jody and Conner.

Jody swept her up in her arms while Conner planted himself between them and the danger. He drew a slow breath and then explained the situation to Jennifer. "I understand that you're upset, Ms. Stewart, but here's the thing. Ms. Kruse has legal custody of Amelia. You know we're not allowed to hand her over without getting permission from her caseworker and the detective in charge of the case."

He tilted his head to the side for a second. "And if you listen carefully, you will hear sirens in the distance. I promise you that they are headed this way. I know because I called them myself."

He waited to give Jennifer a chance to hear the sirens for herself. "The bottom line is that you need to put that gun down now so there are no unfortunate misunderstandings when they arrive."

Jody prayed help would arrive soon. Despite both of their best efforts, there were no indications that Jennifer was going to back down, even though Conner kept trying. "I understand why you're upset, Ms. Stewart. You've obviously been missing Amelia. Anyone would. She's a very special little girl. But believe me, this is not the way to regain custody of her. It only complicates things for everybody."

Jennifer still wasn't buying his arguments. "Listen carefully, Deputy. This isn't complicated at all. Either Amelia comes with me right now or everyone here dies. She's mine or no one's. Don't make me do this."

As if to emphasize that last point, she sighted down the barrel of her gun, aiming right at Conner. Jody fought the urge to scream, fearing the slightest mistake would startle Jennifer into pulling the trigger. Instead, Jody prayed like she'd never prayed before for God's guidance and for Him to help Jennifer Stewart to feel the healing peace of His love. It would take nothing short of a miracle to get them through this moment so fraught with danger.

A second later, Jody caught an unexpected movement out of the corner of her eye that instantly made it easier to breathe. Unexpected help was much closer than the approaching reinforcements that Conner had called for.

It was Mutt. Smart dog that he was, he must have jumped the fence from Conner's yard into hers and then circled around to the far side of her house to jump the fence on that side to reach her front yard. He stalked forward silently as he approached his quarry from behind. It was a team effort as his owner made every effort to keep their target's attention focused solely on himself. It was almost impossible not to stare at the dog as he kept coming, but she didn't want to alert the volatile lady to the threat Mutt presented.

Then, when the dog was less than twenty feet from Jennifer, Conner shouted a word that Jody didn't understand, but Mutt sure did. Between one heartbeat and the next, Mutt launched himself airborne. The huge dog hit Jennifer in the back, knocking her forward and down onto her knees. Everything worked perfectly—until she dropped the gun, which went off at the same time Conner charged forward to join in the fray.

Jody screamed as he collapsed, the right leg of his khakis already turning red as blood gushed from the bullet wound.

SEVENTEEN

Everything became a blur. Before Jody could set Mia down and reach Conner's side, he was already back up and moving. Despite his injury, he continued to fight Jennifer Stewart's attempts to break free. In short order, he had her flipped on her stomach with her arms twisted behind her back. Jody didn't know where the handcuffs had come from, but he quickly snapped them in place. Whatever he said to Mutt had the dog calming down enough to leave his side and head toward Jody and Mia.

After a brief hesitation, Jody released her hold on the little girl. "Go over and sit down on Conner's porch. Take Mutt with you."

The pair did as they were told, leaving Jody free to help Conner. "How badly are you hurt?"

He was pale and breathing hard. Nevertheless, he claimed, "I'll live."

She really hoped so, because the amount of blood on the pavement by his leg was freaking her out. Dropping down beside him, she peeled off her sweatshirt and pressed it against his leg. "The police have arrived. There's also an ambulance stopped farther down the street."

Meanwhile, two officers cautiously circled around behind Jennifer's SUV with their weapons drawn while two more came around from the front. Conner looked back over his shoulder at the sound of their approach and called out, "The suspect is contained."

Despite being in obvious pain, he gave them a succinct summary of the situation. Nodding toward Jody, he said, "This is my neighbor Jody Kruse. She has been fostering the little girl found abandoned at the hospital. Mia is sitting over on my porch cuddling with my dog, Mutt. He's a retired K-9 dog, so approach him carefully. He's probably feeling pretty protective of her right now."

Jennifer was back to screaming for them to turn over Amelia to her. Instead, two of the deputies hauled her up off the ground and ushered her into the back seat of their squad car. Meanwhile, one of the other deputies signaled for EMTs to join the party. When they came running, Jody left Conner to their care. "I'm not going far, but I need to check on Mia."

Conner nodded. "Go. Both she and Mutt will do better with you there."

She felt guilty leaving him, but he was right. Since she was pretty sure they'd be hauling him off to the hospital as soon as they could, she turned back to say one more thing. "Thank you, Conner. For everything."

He remained pretty shaky but obviously determined to do his job. He offered her a brief smile and then resumed his report, bringing his fellow officers up to speed on everything that had happened. From where Jody sat on his front porch with her arms around both Mia and Mutt, she could see Conner was still talking when they loaded him on a gurney and whisked him off to the hospital.

A few minutes later, she was dimly aware of someone walking up the driveway but stopping short of where she and her companions sat huddled together. She lifted her gaze and was relieved to see it was Detective Galloway.

"It's finally over, Detective."

"So I hear." He inched a little closer and squatted down to her eye level. "How are you three doing?"

She tightened her arm around Mia's shoulders. "We've been better, but I'm more concerned about Conner. I know it's too soon for any news about his condition. But when we're done here, I'd appreciate a ride to the hospital if someone can take us. That woman slashed my tires, so my car isn't drivable. I need to be there for him."

"I'll take you myself when I hear he can have visitors." He studied her for a second. "I'm guessing you'll probably want to change clothes before we go."

Then he stood back up and held out his hand to help her up off the porch. "Why don't we walk back over to your house? I'll make you a cup of tea while you get cleaned up."

She glanced down at her clothes and groaned. Both her shirt and pants were covered in blood. Conner's blood. The reminder of how badly he'd been hurt hit her hard. Although she took the detective's hand, she said, "Give me a minute. I might be a little woozy."

Galloway called back over his shoulder, "We'll need an EMT to check out Ms. Kruse after I take her next door."

She looked past him toward the cluster of vehicles out on the street. "I thought they left with Conner."

"They did, but we called for a second ambulance. The woman is claiming she was mauled by a dog and plans to sue everyone she can think of." The man sounded disgusted. "They've checked her over. She has a small bruise on her wrist and a skinned knee. They'll be taking her to the hospital for further evaluation in a few minutes."

At least Jody could help them with one little detail. "For the record, it was Mia who bit that woman on the wrist while trying to get away from her."

The detective grinned and looked down at Mia. "Good for you, kiddo. That was very brave."

Feeling slightly better, Jody let him help her stand. "Mia, would you bring Mutt with us? He'll need to stay with us until Conner can come back home. I also think we could both use something to drink, and I should call Dr. Mayberry to let her know why we've missed our appointment time."

Detective Galloway led their small parade past the

other officers back over to her house. Mutt automatically put himself between Mia and all the strangers. One of the EMTs picked up her bag and followed them up the driveway as two others loaded Jennifer Stewart into a waiting ambulance.

As soon as they shut the door, the tension Jody had been living with for the past couple of weeks eased considerably. There might still be some rough waters ahead for all concerned, but at least Mia was safe. That was all that mattered.

Hopefully, Conner would recover from his wound with no lasting effects, but she hated how close they'd all come to disaster. God had definitely been watching over all of them today.

Once inside the house, she said, "Mia, why don't you and Mutt go look at books in your room? I'm going to change clothes and then bring you both some treats. I think you both deserve extras for being so brave today."

She waited until they were out of sight to join the EMT and Detective Galloway in the kitchen. It didn't take long to get her vitals checked and get the EMT's assessment on the situation: "You seem fine except for a few bruises. Take acetaminophen for any aches or pains. Put ice on the big bruise on your arm and don't hesitate to follow up with your own doctor."

"Thank you. I will."

When the woman packed up and left, Jody turned her attention to the patiently waiting detective. "After

I grab some snacks for Mia and Mutt, I'd like to take a shower and change clothes. Is that okay?"

He nodded. "Anything you need, Jody. Meanwhile, I'll put the kettle on."

"I shouldn't be long."

After getting out some treats, she started toward Mia's room. She'd gone only a few steps when it occurred to her there were some things the detective might want to know as soon as possible. "I don't know if you heard what Conner told the other officers. Just in case, Mia's real name is Amelia Douglas and her father's name was Philip. That woman's name is Jennifer Stewart, and she claims to be Mia's mother. She said that Philip had tried to hide Mia from her. I think she's probably the reason he left Mia at the hospital."

The detective was quickly jotting down notes as she walked away.

Despite the heavy hit of painkillers they'd given him earlier, Conner hurt. The drugs also made him feel thickheaded, which he hated. The last time the nurse had stopped by to check on him, he'd lied and told her he was doing fine. The truth was he'd rather live with the pain and be able to think straight. He'd need his wits about him to deal with the unavoidable aftermath of getting himself shot in the line of duty.

At least they'd given him a private room. He had more important things on his mind than making idle chitchat with some stranger. Stuff like worrying about how Mia, Mutt and Jody were doing. He knew Jody would see to it that Mutt was cared for until Conner got back home to take over. The dog deserved a medal or even a big T-bone steak for what he'd done. Jody had kept her head, too. He was proud of them both, and he'd never forget little Mia chomping on Jennifer Stewart's arm like that.

Jody and Mia both had the kind of strength that it took to be a cop's family. Funny how getting shot could make a man realize what was important in life. He probably shouldn't be thinking this way, but he couldn't imagine a future without Jody in it. And, God willing, they could offer a permanent home to Mia. Amelia. Whatever she wanted to be called.

The truth of all that settled in his heart. Now he needed to find the right words and the courage to tell Jody how much he'd come to love her. Looking back, it had started that first night, when she'd tried desperately to comfort a terrified child, and had only grown every day since. He could only pray that she felt the same about him.

A knock at the door startled him out of his reverie. Evidently, he had an actual visitor. Doctors and nurses might knock first, but then they waltzed on in without waiting for permission. "Come in."

Jack Galloway stuck his head in the door. "You up for some company? I come bearing gifts—good coffee and sugary treats."

Bless him for that. The hospital food was pretty decent, but the coffee was almost as bad as the stuff from the vending machine at work. "Sure, come on in."

He pressed the button that would raise the head of the bed to put himself on more even footing with his guest. At the same time, the detective pulled a chair up near the side of the bed and sat down. He passed Conner one of the coffees and put two enormous apple fritters on napkins within easy reach on the table. "I'd ask how you're doing, but you're as white as that sheet. Besides, you'd only lie and say you're fine and dandy."

"Yeah, I would." Conner grinned at him. "To tell the truth, my stitches itch and my leg really hurts. They'd give me something to help with that if I asked, but I hate the way drugs make me feel. That said, I'll let them dose me up later so I can sleep tonight. I'm not a complete idiot."

"Yeah, you should get all the rest you can." Jack sipped his coffee and set it aside. "I won't stay long, but I hear you'll only be here another day max before they kick you to the curb. I've already volunteered to come take you home."

Actually, Conner had been thinking about calling Jody, but it might be simpler to accept Jack's offer. Jody had both Mia and Mutt to consider. "I'd appreciate it. I'll call you when I know more."

"Do that."

Conner studied the older man. He looked tired but more relaxed than the last few times he'd seen him. "So it's over."

"Yeah, it is. I thought you'd like to hear firsthand what I've learned in the past few hours." Without waiting for Conner to respond, he launched right in. "Mia's real name is Amelia Douglas. Her father was Philip Douglas, a college professor from over in the Seattle area. Apparently, he'd recently taken an unexpected sabbatical, which explains in part why no one was looking for him. From what we've been told, his wife died from a sudden illness shortly after the little girl was born. Mia never knew the woman."

"That makes sense considering her response when Jody had asked her about her mother. So who was Jennifer Stewart if not Mia's mother?"

Jack leaned back in his chair and took another sip of his coffee. "That's where things get weird. The details are still coming in, but apparently she was sort of their combination nanny and housekeeper. The agency that sent her claims she had excellent references that checked out when she listed with them. We don't know what happened, but somewhere along the line Ms. Stewart decided that she wanted to be more than the nanny. From what we can gather, she somehow got it into her head that Philip was her husband and the little girl was her actual daughter. Not sure what all happened after that, but it wasn't anything good. Seems Philip fired her about two months ago and right after that got a restraining order against her."

Conner clenched his hands into tight fists. No wonder little Mia had been so scared of the woman.

"She must have upped the ante big-time if he went on the run like that. Using a false identity and everything else he did was pretty extreme."

The detective closed his eyes for several seconds before responding. "Yeah, it was. For the life of me, I can't figure out why he didn't call the police about what was going on. All things considered, we may never know all the details about what his thinking was. At least the suspect has already admitted that she shot him before running him off the road. I expect ballistics to confirm that the gun she had with her today is the same one she used to shoot Mr. Douglas. Regardless, she wounded a cop, assaulted Jody and attempted to kidnap Mia. Adding all of that to murder charges, she's going to be behind bars for a very long time."

Conner shifted, trying to find a more comfortable position for his aching leg. "I almost feel sorry for her. I hope they can get her whatever kind of help she needs—not that I think she belongs back out on the street in the foreseeable future, or maybe ever."

Because nothing excused what Jennifer Stewart had done. At least both Mia and Jody were safe now. Which brought Conner back to a question he was almost afraid to ask. "What's going to happen to Mia?"

Jack shrugged. "That's up to the courts. I talked to Dale Greve. They'll search for any close relatives, but that stuff takes time. The good news is that until CPS has definite answers, Mia will be staying with Jody."

Then Jack stood up. "And speaking of those two,

they're pacing the hall outside waiting for their turn to see you. I drove them here, but I asked them to give me the first shot. I'll be parked out in the waiting room until they're ready to go back home."

Then he opened the door. "Okay, ladies. He's all yours."

He stood back out of the way while Mia led the charge into the room. She looked adorable in pink sweats and her hair done up in pigtails with bows to match her outfit. As soon as she spotted him, her face lit up with a big grin. She ran across to stand by the bed and held up her arms.

"Sorry, little one. I'd really love a hug, but I can't pick you up. The doctors told me to stay really still today so I can come home tomorrow."

Jody had joined her small charge standing beside the bed. "Mia, I can lift you up, but you'll have to be gentle when you hug Conner."

Conner gritted his teeth as he scooted a few inches toward the far side of his bed to make room. "Let's give it a shot."

Jody carefully picked up Mia and set her on the edge of the bed. The little girl moved slowly to wrap her arms around Conner's neck and laid her head against his chest. He smiled as he enfolded her in his arms. Even if he wasn't sure which of them needed the contact more, it felt good to hold her close knowing she was finally safe. After he pressed a kiss to the top of Mia's head, Jody carried her over to sit in the chair that Jack had recently vacated.

Then she returned to stand beside the bed. "Now it's my turn."

His heart did a slow roll as he held his arms out to her. He was pretty sure she was crying, but that was okay. She'd probably been putting on a brave front for Mia's sake, but the whole experience had been traumatic for all concerned.

Conner gently stroked her back with one hand and threaded the fingers of his other one into the wild curls of her hair. "I promise I'm okay, Jody. The bullet missed hitting anything important. It was a through and through, so the doctors only needed to clean the wounds and then stitch them up."

She lifted her head and looked at him with eyes glistening with tears. "You lost so much blood."

Mustering up a crooked smile, he did his best to reassure her. "They topped off my tank with a bunch of fluids and put me on antibiotics as a precaution. I can also take something for pain if I need to."

Still cuddled in close, she asked, "How soon will you be able to go back to work?"

"It's too soon to tell. I'm guessing I may have to be on light duty for a little while. That usually means working at a desk instead of going out on patrol."

When she finally shifted to perch on the edge of the bed, he liked that she maintained contact with him by placing her hand over his heart. "Thank you for everything you've done for us all this time. I'm not sure we would've survived without you."

He really didn't need her to thank him for doing his job, but it was still nice. "I'm glad I was able to help."

She grabbed a tissue from the box on his bedside table and swiped away the tears on her cheeks. Even with red eyes and a sniffly nose, she was so amazingly beautiful to him.

"Even though it got you shot?"

"Even though." He brushed a lock of her hair back behind her ear. "It was all worth it, because it brought you into my life." Then he caught her hand in his and kissed it. "Fair warning—I don't want us to go back to being the kind of neighbors who wave when we happen to see each other."

He glanced past her to where Mia sat watching them. "It's been twenty years since I was part of a normal family, but I'm thinking I'd like to build a new one with you. And if pigtails over there needs a permanent home, I want us to be the ones who give it to her."

Just that quickly, Jody's tears were back, but the expression on her face was far happier. "I want that, too, but I was afraid it was too soon to be thinking that way."

She slowly leaned in close to brush her lips across his. Conner immediately gave in to the temptation to pull her closer and do a proper job of kissing her. Jody was blushing as she stood up, but that was okay. "We'll talk more when I get home tomorrow. If you need time, I'll try to be patient."

Her answering smile was everything he could have

hoped for. "I don't think you'll have to wait all that long, Conner. I thank God every day for bringing you into our lives."

Then she glanced at the clock on the wall. "The nurse recommended we keep our visit short. You need your rest, so we should get going. Jack already said he would bring you home tomorrow. I hope that's okay, because I think he really wants to do something for you. But once you get there, Mia, Mutt and I will be on hand to take care of you."

He threaded his fingers through hers, wanting to keep her close as long as possible. "You'll spoil me rotten, and I'm going to let you."

That made her laugh. "There's one more thing. Before we go, Mia saw something in the gift shop downstairs and insisted that you needed it."

She pointed toward a bag sitting on the floor by the door. "Mia, why don't you give him his present before the nurse comes to kick us out?"

The little girl scrambled down out of the chair to get the bag. She waited until she was standing right by the bed to do the big reveal. She proudly held up a stuffed toy that looked an awful lot like a certain German shepherd. Conner gently took it from her hand. "Thank you, Mia. Now I won't be lonely when I sleep tonight."

Then she rose up on her toes to get closer to Conner and proudly whispered two words. "It's Mutt!"

EPILOGUE

Six months later

The church was filled to capacity, a mix of friends, family and coworkers. Pastor Dahl moved to stand at the front as Conner and his best man took their positions. The organist struck a chord and began playing.

Mia appeared at the back of the church carrying a small bouquet of daisies and wearing a bright blue dress and black patent leather shoes. Conner couldn't help but grin as she started down the aisle, carefully walking in step with her four-legged escort. When they reached the front of the church, she stepped to the left as Mutt went right to stand between Conner and Justin, his former handler.

Once they were all in place, the organist launched into the wedding march. Everyone looked toward the back of the church where Conner's bride now stood. Jody's smile was huge as Papa Burks offered her his arm. The pair took their own sweet time finding their way to where Conner stood waiting. He knew he should be patient, but he'd been waiting for this day for months—maybe his whole life. It was time he and Jody announced their love for each other in front of God and everyone else who had come to celebrate the occasion.

At long last, Jody reached his side, and Conner took her hand in his. That small connection calmed his nerves as the pastor began to talk. "We are gathered here in God's house to witness the marriage of Jody Kruse and Conner Dunne."

From that point, the ceremony flowed smoothly. After they finally exchanged their vows, Pastor Dahl beamed at both of them as he signaled for Mia to move over to stand between them. When she was in position, he made a surprise announcement. "I am so pleased to say that this occasion is even more special than any of you know. I wish to thank everyone who worked behind the scenes to help make this final part of the ceremony possible. Now, with the assistance of the Honorable Judge Davis Lebart, we will finalize the adoption of Amelia 'Mia' Douglas by Conner and Jody Dunne."

The judge first congratulated them on their marriage and then led them through the formalities of making Mia officially their daughter. When everything was finished, he signed the paperwork with a flourish and grinned. "Conner, Jody and Mia, I now pronounce you a family."

A ripple of laughter and applause swept through the church. The pastor gave everyone time to settle down before continuing. "So let us all bow our heads to give thanks and offer blessings for this new family."

When it was over, the three humans and their furry companion walked down the aisle and into their future together.

* * * * *

Get 4 FREE REWARDS!

We'll send you 2 FREE Books plus 2 FREE Mystery Gifts.

FREE Value Over **$20**

Both the **Harlequin® Special Edition** and **Harlequin® Heartwarming™** series feature compelling novels filled with stories of love and strength where the bonds of friendship, family and community unite.

YES! Please send me 2 FREE novels from the Harlequin Special Edition or Harlequin Heartwarming series and my 2 FREE gifts (gifts are worth about $10 retail). After receiving them, if I don't wish to receive any more books, I can return the shipping statement marked "cancel." If I don't cancel, I will receive 6 brand-new Harlequin Special Edition books every month and be billed just $5.49 each in the U.S. or $6.24 each in Canada, a savings of at least 12% off the cover price, or 4 brand-new Harlequin Heartwarming Larger-Print books every month and be billed just $6.24 each in the U.S. or $6.74 each in Canada, a savings of at least 19% off the cover price. It's quite a bargain! Shipping and handling is just 50¢ per book in the U.S. and $1.25 per book in Canada.* I understand that accepting the 2 free books and gifts places me under no obligation to buy anything. I can always return a shipment and cancel at any time by calling the number below. The free books and gifts are mine to keep no matter what I decide.

Choose one: ☐ **Harlequin Special Edition**
(235/335 HDN GRJV)

☐ **Harlequin Heartwarming Larger-Print**
(161/361 HDN GRJV)

Name (please print)

Address   Apt. #

City   State/Province   Zip/Postal Code

Email: Please check this box ☐ if you would like to receive newsletters and promotional emails from Harlequin Enterprises ULC and its affiliates. You can unsubscribe anytime.

Mail to the Harlequin Reader Service:
IN U.S.A.: P.O. Box 1341, Buffalo, NY 14240-8531
IN CANADA: P.O. Box 603, Fort Erie, Ontario L2A 5X3

Want to try 2 free books from another series! Call 1-800-873-8635 or visit www.ReaderService.com.

*Terms and prices subject to change without notice. Prices do not include sales taxes, which will be charged (if applicable) based on your state or country of residence. Canadian residents will be charged applicable taxes. Offer not valid in Quebec. This offer is limited to one order per household. Books received may not be as shown. Not valid for current subscribers to the Harlequin Special Edition or Harlequin Heartwarming series. All orders subject to approval. Credit or debit balances in a customer's account(s) may be offset by any other outstanding balance owed by or to the customer. Please allow 4 to 6 weeks for delivery. Offer available while quantities last.

Your Privacy—Your information is being collected by Harlequin Enterprises ULC, operating as Harlequin Reader Service. For a complete summary of the information we collect, how we use this information and to whom it is disclosed, please visit your privacy notice located at corporate.harlequin.com/privacy-notice. From time to time we may also exchange your personal information with reputable third parties. If you wish to opt out of this sharing of your personal information, please visit readerservice.com/consumerchoice or call 1-800-873-8635. **Notice to California Residents**—Under California law, you have specific rights to control and access your data. For more information on these rights and how to exercise them, visit corporate.harlequin.com/california-privacy.

HSEHW22R3

Get 4 FREE REWARDS!

We'll send you 2 FREE Books <u>plus</u> 2 FREE Mystery Gifts.

FREE Value Over **$20**

Both the **Worldwide Library** and **Essential Suspense** series feature compelling novels filled with gripping mysteries, edge of your seat thrillers and heart-stopping romantic suspense stories.

HARLEQUIN
PLUS

Try the best multimedia subscription service for romance readers like you!

Read, Watch and Play.

Experience the easiest way to get the romance content you crave.

Start your **FREE TRIAL** at
<u>www.harlequinplus.com/freetrial</u>.